Timing...The Key to Life

A novel set in Roswell, Georgia

Also by Morgan Rodgers:

<u>One Line Management</u> – a reference of easy to find quotes, conveniently arranged in chapters for the "one in charge". Always be prepared to say the right thing at the right time.

Timing...
The Key to Life

Morgan Rodgers

Morgan Rodgers

Timing…The Key to Life

ISBN-10 1452853053
ISBN-13 978-1452853055

Credits

Editor: Jade Rodgers

Printed in the United States of America

This book is dedicated:

To my wife, Janet; she is absolutely the best person I have ever known. Thanks for supporting me for all these years, even when I did not deserve it. And thanks for asking, at last count a million times, "Why don't you write a book?" See, I do listen.

To my kids, Colby and Jade; thank you for putting up with my sense of humor all these years. Both of your insights, while completely different, help me get through it all.

A special thanks to my editor for telling me she enjoyed the story, every time she read it.

Morgan Rodgers

Chapter 1

Tuesday

What would you do if you won $250,000,000? That was the question on everyone's mind as the Georgia State Lottery's Mega Millions game jackpot hit its largest total ever.

The Corner Grocery, at the corner of Woodstock Street and Canton Street, was the place of choice to buy lottery tickets for many of the City of Roswell employees. It was 5:20 pm on a typical Tuesday afternoon in mid-January and the line to buy the life-changing tickets was growing.

Most of those in the line of millionaire want-to-bes were from either the City's Public Works Department or the Recreation and Parks Department.

"I'd move to Aruba and never be cold again," claimed Bart Henderson. Bart was the long time crew leader at the city's flagship Park, the Roswell Area Park. It had been an exceptionally cold day in Georgia as the temperature struggled to reach 30 degrees. Bart always liked to lead his crew by example both in the physical sense and the mental part. Today he had struggled to keep himself and his crew positive as they repaired a water leak, and because of their hard work, hundreds of kids were enjoying gymnastic and dance classes at the Physical Activity Center at this very moment. They had temporarily repaired the water line, but would have to finish the full repair tomorrow when the temperature was supposed to get above freezing.

"Not me," said Chris Lamar, "I'd buy them sorry ass Atlanta Hawks and build them a new stadium here on the north side of town so I wouldn't have to ride MARTA just to see a game." Chris was a sports fan in the biggest way. His favorite sport was the one that was being played. "Then I would go pay that Labron fellow enough to come to Atlanta and I would have me a NBA Championship."

Chris worked as a street sweeper for the City Public Works Department. Chris was raised in Roswell and took great pride in the fact that what he did helped to make Roswell one of the cleanest, prettiest cities in Georgia.

"I'd run for mayor and promise everyone I would pay their city taxes if I was elected." This remark came from Wade Farmer, a 15-year veteran of the Public Works

Department. "Then when I was elected, I'd fire Walker, that son of a bitch." Joe Walker, Wade's supervisor, had denied his request to be off work on Saturday; Wade had wanted to go hunting.

I'd have to split it 71 ways, thought Stone Lee. Stone worked at the Roswell Area Park. He spent most of his 40 hours each week repairing water lines, irrigation systems and plumbing problems. The park offered 13 athletic fields, a large recreation center, a gymnastics and dance center, a visual arts center, 12 tennis courts, a 3-mile lighted jogging trail, an Olympic-sized swimming pool, a large, shaded playground and numerous outdoor restroom facilities. Stone stayed busy.

It was Stone's turn to buy the tickets for the lottery group he and some of his coworkers assembled every time the jackpot got over $100,000,000. The deal was anyone could buy a share in the pool for $1 per share. Each share would get an equal amount of the jackpot if they hit all five numbers plus the Mega Millions ball.

The group members took turns buying the tickets. Whoever's turn it was had to write down how much each of their "partners" had given them and then buy the tickets at the Corner Grocery. There were a total of 71 shares this week: Carter King had 25 shares, Pee Wee Cooper had 15, Bart Henderson had 10, Justin Turner had 10, Will Wall had 5 and Mark Sloan had 5; Stone had only one.

Stone was in a hurry as usual. He had asked Bart to buy the tickets for him earlier in the day since Bart always stopped at the Corner Grocery after work. "No way," hissed Bart when Stone asked for his help. "It's your turn and your responsibility. I'm not doing your job for you." Bart always played strictly by the rules.

As a single dad raising two kids it seemed that Stone did not have enough time to do the things he had to do, much less anything he wanted to do. His oldest, Steven, had a basketball game at East Roswell Park that started at 6:30 pm that evening.

East Roswell Park was on the other side of Georgia 400, which meant more traffic than Stone wanted to think about. He had not had time to go by the bank and get cash. He only had $1 to put in the pool for himself.

It'll be just my luck that we will win and I will only have one share, Stone thought.

Finally it was Stone's turn in line. Andrew, who owned the Corner Grocery along with his mother and father, was a good natured fellow with an Asian accent. "How do I help you today, Stone?"

"I need 71 quick picks for tonight's Mega Millions," Stone instructed Andrew. Quick picks simply meant that the computer randomly picked the numbers. The computer spat out the numbers in quick succession. Seven slips with 10 sets of numbers each and one slip with one set of numbers.

"I hope you win," laughed Andrew. "I need the money." The Georgia Lottery paid their distribution sites a bonus if they sold winning tickets.

"Not as bad as I do," Stone said. *If only they knew,* he thought.

Stone knew if he did not hurry his son would be late for his basketball game, which meant Steven would not play in the first quarter and he would be mad at his father for the rest of the night.

Stone hated being late. He always thought that people who were late were being disrespectful.

He slipped the numbers into his shirt pocket and headed toward the Waller Park Recreation Center to pick up his kids from the after school program that the YMCA ran in cooperation with the city. Stone hoped that Steven had remembered to bring his basketball jersey.

Chapter 2

Tuesday

Stone loved his kids more than he could explain. His wife had felt the same way. They were the happiest family in Roswell, Georgia. To sum it up, life was good, real good.

Kathy, Stone's wife, was his best friend, soul mate; they were a match made in heaven. Nothing could tear them apart, or so they thought. Then the cancer arrived.

Kathy was the bravest person Stone had ever known. She had battled several different types of cancer in various parts of her body. She had gone through chemotherapy and radiation, had taken all kinds of drugs and had even gone to Mexico to try an experimental type of treatment that had not yet been authorized in the United States. But, in the end, the cancer had won. Stone could not believe that it had been two years since Kathy had died in his arms. With her last breath she said, "Stone, do whatever it takes to take care of our kids." He had promised her he would, and then she smiled and silently slipped away.

Now, Stone's only connection to Kathy was his two kids, Steven and Paula. Steven was quite a sight to see. He had good looks, lots of brains, and natural athletic ability. He obviously got his looks and his brains from Kathy, but the athletic ability came from Stone. Steven was a natural at every sport he tried. Already at age 14 he was on track to be showered by scholarships from his choice of colleges. Stone secretly hoped that he would choose to play basketball at Clemson University. That had been Stone's dream when he was in high school, but a knee injury the summer after he graduated ended that aspiration.

Paula was another story. She had inherited her natural beauty from Kathy. Of course, just like Kathy, she did not believe she was pretty, even though everyone told her so. But in addition to her beauty she also inherited Kathy's constant struggle to stay healthy. Paula had asthma, a low white blood cell count and diabetes, all of which could be managed with the right medication, diet, and proper rest.

But the one thing that could not be easily treated and would not go away was the need for a new kidney. Paula had a rare kidney disease, the name of which Stone could not even pronounce, much less understand. Neither Stone nor Steven was a viable candidate for donating a kidney. Of course, Kathy would have been, if she had been alive.

Currently, Paula was on several waiting lists at several different hospitals for a donated kidney. At Emory Hospital in Atlanta, she was number 23 on the list. The doctors had told Stone that at the current rate of transplants, Paula was maybe two to three years away from receiving her donated kidney. However, the Lee family doctor, Dr. Ishmael, told Stone that without a transplant, Paula had no more than 10 months to live.

Timing...the key to life.

While that information was enough to give Stone ulcers, what kept him up at night was knowing that he could take Paula to Mexico and, for the right price, get her a new kidney in a matter of days. According to Dr. Ishmael, there was an underground black market in Mexico for such things. It was safe and very reliable, but also very expensive. Not only because of the medical cost, but also because it would require Stone to move to Mexico for six months to stay with Paula while she recovered from her transplant surgery.

Stone had sat down almost every night to calculate and recalculate the expenses:

Cost of the operation:	$1,500,000
Flights and travel expenses:	$5,000
Missed wages for six months:	$25,000
Room at hotel next to hospital:	$30,000
Food and living expenses:	$25,000
Doctor expenses:	$600,000
Post surgery treatment:	$350,000
Miscellaneous expenses:	$250,000
Payoff of various officials:	$750,000
Grand Total:	**$3,535,000**

Stone knew the figures by heart. His little girl could be saved, but he could not find the way to make it happen. But what kept eating at him was his final promise to his wife to do whatever it took to take care of his children.

Instinctively, Stone reached over and hugged Paula. "I'll find a way," he whispered to himself. "I love you more than you will ever know," he said out loud to Paula.

"Aren't you watching the game, Dad? Steven just made another three-point shot." Paula was pulling away from her dad, obviously worried that someone would see her dad hugging her in public. As a 10-year-old child in the 5th grade at Roswell North Elementary School, she hoped none of the cool kids were watching.

Stone turned his attention to his son, who was looking up at him from the basketball court with a look that said, *"I can't believe you just missed seeing me make that shot!"*

Stone would hear about that from his son on the way home tonight.

Timing... the key to life.

*****

Steven's team, the Hawks, won their 5th straight game that night. The final score was Hawks 34 – Sonics 20. Steven had been in the zone as he scored 23 points, the most he had ever scored in a single game. Despite having such a good night, he was disappointed that his father had not been concentrating on the game. He showed his malcontent by giving Stone the silent treatment on the way home after the game.

They left the East Roswell Recreation Center at 7:45 pm. By the time they got something to eat, did homework, and took baths, it would be bedtime. Stone sighed as he realized it would be another night like so many others had been. Get everything done for the kids, watch the 11:00 pm news, followed by another restless night of little to no sleep.

Chapter 3

Tuesday

Stone and the kids stopped by Slope's BBQ for dinner on the way home from the basketball game. It was on the way, but that's not why they stopped. Everybody in the family liked going to Slope's. Steven favored pulled BBQ pork. Paula liked the grilled cheese sandwich. Stone usually got the vegetable plate because the vegetables tasted just like the ones his mother used to make.

The family ate out a lot. It was easier to go out than to cook and then clean up the kitchen. It was also a lot faster. Stone was up for anything that saved him any time. There were just not enough hours in the day to get all the homework, baths, housework, etc, done.

The kids had been especially good tonight. Paula had done her homework while Steven was playing basketball. She was now quietly playing in her room. Stone took great pleasure in knowing she was happy and content despite her various ailments.

Steven had gone straight to his room and gotten to work on his science project. He was building an exact scale model of the solar system. The project was not due until next Monday and he only had Uranus and Pluto to go. Steven had debated whether to include Pluto or not in the project. Technically, Pluto was not a planet, but he was also including the moons in the project, so he decided to include Pluto. Pluto is, after all, part of our solar system.

Bed time at the Lee house was not set in stone. Paula usually was asleep by 9 pm and Steven by 10 pm. That gave Stone a couple of hours before he went to bed to worry about finances, bills and payments.

Stone barely had enough money to pay all the bills on his salary. The monthly bills alone were high enough: mortgage payment, car payment, utilities, food, credit cards, taxes, insurance, school supplies, and activities for the kids. If that was all there was, they could get by. But it was the medical bills that were slowly but surely putting them under. Even with insurance, the special medical care that Paula required was just too much.

It was slowly driving Stone crazy. The only thing that stood between Paula and a long life was money.

What was he going to do? He could not just let his daughter die.

*****

Sometimes it seemed to Stone that the only break he got was when he watched the nightly news. Tonight he was watching Channel 2, which broadcast the Georgia Lottery results live.

Channel 2, WSB Atlanta, was the official television station for the Georgia State Lottery. Every night at 11:00 pm, immediately before the nightly news, there was a lottery drawing of some sort. On Mondays, Wednesdays and Thursdays the winning numbers for Cash 4 and Fantasy 5 were aired live. On Saturdays the Win For Life drawing was held. This game paid the winning ticket holder $1000 per week for life. But the big money was given away every Tuesday and Friday night with the drawing for Mega Millions.

Whoever's turn it was to buy the tickets for the lottery group was also expected to check the tickets and confirm the fact that the group had again lost. Stone had found the easiest way to verify the numbers was to write them down as they rolled out of the lottery number bin, and then actually check the tickets against the winning numbers later.

With a face made for TV and a smile as big as Stone Mountain, Libby Reynolds, the official Georgia Lottery announcer, was explaining the game. "Hello America. You could be the nation's next millionaire simply by matching all five of tonight's white balls and our gold Mega Millions ball. Good Luck. Tonight's first number is 27. Followed by 12. Next is 15. Then we have 29. Next is 2. Tonight's Mega Millions number is 2. The winning numbers are: 27, 12, 15, 29, 2 and the Mega Millions number is 2. If no one matches tonight's numbers, Friday's jackpot could be worth a record $500,000,000. Good night, good luck and play on Georgia."

The 11:00 pm local news began immediately after the lottery drawing. Channel 2's catch phrase was "Coverage You Can Count On". The news in Atlanta was pretty predictable. Several armed robberies, a scandal in the Georgia Legislature, state revenues down, more workers to be laid off, and at least one shooting a night in downtown Atlanta.

Stone really wanted to know what the weather would be like tomorrow so he would know how to dress the kids and himself since he was going to be outside again fixing that water line break. The thing about the weather in Georgia is that if you don't like the weather, be patient for a few days, it'll change.

Finally, Glen Burns, the perennial weather man in Atlanta, gave the low down on Wednesday's weather. It was going to be a little bit warmer, but not by much. The high temperature would be 34 degrees, with a lot of wind and little to no sunshine. What that meant for Stone was another day when his toes would start out frozen and would get colder as the day went on. At least it was not going to rain. The only thing worse than fixing a water leak in the cold was fixing a water leak in the cold and rain.

Once he got tomorrow's weather forecast, Stone channel-surfed until he found a rerun of "Deal or No Deal". He drifted off to sleep with Howie asking "Deal or No Deal?" Little did he know that, in a few hours, he was going to have to decide if he was going to take the deal or not.

Morgan Rodgers

Chapter 4

Wednesday

The Atlanta Journal Constitution has been the daily newspaper for metro Atlanta since 1868. It is the largest daily newspaper in the Southeast with a daily circulation of 640,000. But now, like many papers across the country, the AJC was experiencing a drop in paper subscriptions. People were going online and reading the newspaper on their computer screens. AJC.com was quickly becoming the site of choice around Atlanta.

Stone was old school. He wanted his morning coffee and morning newspaper. He liked to do what he called "ease into the morning." He got up at 5:30 am so he would have a full hour to himself before the kids got up.

His morning routine had not changed for the last 10 years. First he would get Mr. Coffee going with classic Folgers coffee. Then he would walk up his driveway and pick up the daily AJC. Finally, he would sit at the kitchen table, read the paper, drink his coffee and eat his morning donut.

There would be no easing into this particular morning. Stone almost spit out his Folgers at what he read. The headlines on the front page reported:

Local Wins Largest Jackpot

Just below that appeared:

Roswell Corner Grocery Makes History

Stone could not believe it. The winning ticket was sold at the same place he had bought his tickets. Could it be true?

Timing... the key to life.

Stone almost knocked over the table and chairs as he scrambled to get to the kitchen counter where he had left his tickets. Then he grabbed his notepad by the television remote where he had written down the winning numbers last night.

Experience told Stone to check the Mega Millions numbers first. If you didn't get that number you could win a little cash, but not the big money. He found two number 2's on the tickets.

Two chances to save my little girl's life, he thought. He checked the first number 2 numbers: 7 - 12 - 22 - 21 - 36. One number and the Mega Millions ball. Big deal. That would buy him a six pack of beer and that was about it.

Then the checked the next ticket with 2 as the Mega-Millions ball: 2 - 12 - 15 - 27 - 29.

Holy shit, Stone thought. He took a deep breath and checked the numbers again. 2 - 12 - 15 - 27 - 29.

"Holy shit," this time he said it out loud. As luck would have it, Paula walked in just as Stone said the "s" word.

"What did you just say?" asked Paula in that condescending way a child can ask a question of a parent when the elder has done something they should not have done. "I didn't think we were supposed to use that word."

"Sorry darling," Stone said automatically. "I just hit my toe on the table. I'll be more careful what I say next time."

This can't be right, Stone thought. *This kind of stuff does not happen to me. Calm down, Stone*, he kept saying to himself. *You probably wrote the numbers down wrong.*

Trying to keep his emotions in check, he reached for the phone and called the Georgia State Lottery's hotline information service. Anyone that played the Georgia Lottery regularly knew the number by heart. But Stone's heart was racing so fast he had to think. Slowly, the phone number came to him.

He waited for the answer. "You have reached the Georgia State Lottery player information line. Please listen carefully, as the menu has recently changed. For directions to the Georgia State Lottery Office, press one. For all winning results, press two." Stone's hands were shaking so much that it was hard for him to hit the right button, but he did. "For current Mega Millions results, press one."

"OK, here goes," Stone said, taking a deep breath and trying to calm himself.

"The winning Mega Millions numbers for Tuesday, January 12th are: 2, 12, 15, 27, 29 and the Mega Millions number is 2. Thank you for calling the Georgia State Lottery player information line."

Stone did not know how to react. The lottery group had won. They were rich. They were millionaires. He could save his child.

He could save his baby girl.

Stone's shaking was almost uncontrollable now. He had to call everyone. For some reason he wondered who would fix the water leak since all the guys at the park were filthy rich and would not be going to work today.

Should he try to call everyone now or wait and tell everyone when they got to work? Thoughts were coming and going too quickly for Stone to figure things out.

He finally sat in his chair and starting calming down. How much had they won? He remembered the amount in the newspaper article. The jackpot was $250,000,000 dollars.

But that amount was based on the jackpot being annuitized. That meant that the jackpot would be paid over the course of 20 years, an equal amount paid each year. But the group had already decided that if they ever won they would not take the annuitized prize, but rather the cash option. The cash option would reduce the jackpot significantly. Stone did not know by how much, but he had heard that between taxes and the cash option that winners usually received about half of the annuitized jackpot.

That meant that the $250,000,000 suddenly went to $125,000,000. That is still a lot of money, but suddenly Stone realized that he had only bought one share and that there were 70 other shares. Stone could not tell if it was panic or fear that ran through his veins. Whatever it was, he did not like it. He forced himself to walk slowly over to the cabinet drawer that held all the bills, as well as the calculator. He plugged in 125,000,000 and then divided that by 71. The answer he dreaded flashed up on the little screen: $1,760,563.38.

Not enough. Almost $2,000,000.00 short of the $3,535,000.00 he needed for Paula's operation. He felt the blood drain from his head. He had to sit down. As he did, he almost missed his chair, but caught himself at the last minute as the chair scooted back.

Steven was walked into the kitchen and said, "What's up, Dad? You look like you just saw a ghost."

Stone did not hear his son. He could not stop staring at the calculator. How could he win the lottery and it not be enough?

Steven repeated himself, this time a little louder and with attitude, "What's up Dad? You look like you just saw a ghost."

Now Paula was in the kitchen and she jumped right into the fray. "Dad, if I talked to you like that, you would yell at me."

Stone was slowly coming out of his funk. "Sorry kids, I just thought I had more money than I do." Then, realizing what he had said, he attempted a recovery with "Same stuff, different day."

Steven said, "I can get a part time job at Publix and make some money. You know the manager there, don't you?" Steven was trying to become more independent and Stone was not sure if he liked that or not.

"No way are you working at your age. All this means is that I won't be able to buy that new golf club I wanted."

The kids just shrugged. Basically telling their dad without saying it out loud, *whatever*.

The kids got their own breakfast. Paula favored bagels and cream cheese, while Steven liked Cinnamon Toast Crunch. Maybe not the best breakfasts, but at least they weren't eating sugar coated donuts like their dad.

*****

Stone always took both kids to school on his way to work at Roswell Area Park. From their house on Wave Tree Drive, it only took a couple of minutes to make the circuit to Crabapple Middle School, Roswell North Elementary School and the Roswell Area Park.

The radio in Stone's 1998 Isuzu Trooper was always on country music. During their short drive in the morning, the Lee family always listened to their favorite D.J, Moby in the Morning. Moby was an institution in Atlanta morning radio. He had spent many years as the top radio personality at several of Atlanta's big country radio stations. His trademark phrase was "Yea, Baby".

A few years earlier, Moby had broken away from the mainstream radio and started his own syndicated radio show which he entitled "The Biggest Small Town in America". Currently he is the morning personality for many small town market radio stations around the Southeast. 106.1 in Athens, Georgia is part of Moby's radio family and it came in crystal clear in Roswell.

This morning, even Moby was talking about the lottery winner. "If the winner is listening," Moby declared, "if you need a financial advisor, all you got to do is call your old pal Mr. Moby. I will take care of your money so you won't ever have to worry again. For a small price, that is. Yea Baby."

Stone smiled and thought, *Maybe a spokesperson would not be a bad idea.* Moby, never at a loss for words, could answer all the questions. Stone sure didn't want to.

As Stone dropped Steven off at Crabapple Middle School, Steven looked oddly at his dad and said, "You seem extra weird today, Dad. Are you sure you are alright?"

Stone looked at his oldest child and saw the worry in the young man's eyes. "Yeah, I am fine son. Just a lot on my plate right now. Don't worry. Have a good day. I love you, son."

"Love you too, Dad."

*****

The drive from Crabapple Middle to Roswell North Elementary School was a short one, but the traffic was especially heavy this morning. At the corner of Crabapple and Woodstock, as Stone was making a right, he could see why. The Corner Grocery was a hub of activity. On site were Channel 2, Channel 46, Channel 5 and Channel 11, all the local television stations. There was even a van from CNN. This worldwide news agency had its headquarters in Atlanta.

The whole world was watching the Corner Grocery in Roswell. Two questions were on everyone's mind: Who had won the money? And what were they going to do with it?

*****

Roswell North Elementary School was no more than half a mile down Woodstock Road from the Corner Grocery. The school sat right next to the Roswell Area Park where Stone worked. He pulled into the drop-off lane and was content to just wait his turn in silence.

Paula had other ideas. "You know Dad, Steven was right. You are acting weird. You seem to be a million miles away. I don't like it when you are quiet and don't talk to me. It's like I'm not here."

At that very moment, Stone knew what he must do.

He turned to look at Paula, sitting in the back seat, and said, "I'm sorry, baby. I have been distant lately, because I had so many problems that I could not solve. But all of that is behind us now. Things are going to get much better real soon. We're going to get you well so you can live a good life. How would you like that?"

Paula, always the realist said, "Dad, I love you. I know you will take care of me. I know we will be happy as long as we have each other. See ya." And she was out the door.

Stone just watched her walk up the steps to the school. So young, so pretty, so full of love and so sick.

Kathy's words filled the car, "Stone, do whatever it takes to take care of our kids."

"I will, I promise," Stone said out loud even though there was no one in the car with him.

The soccer mom behind him obviously had a tennis match to get to as she blew the horn much longer than was necessary.

Realizing that he was holding up the entire drop-off line, Stone put his Trooper into drive and headed back to the Corner Grocery. The plan was set in his mind. He had to make a quick purchase.

Chapter 5

Wednesday

Because of his unscheduled visit to the Corner Grocery, Stone was running late to work. That was unusual for him. He had always thought that being on time meant you were already late. With him being late, he was sure the lottery group at the maintenance shop had convinced themselves they had won. What other reason could there be for Stone to be late?

As he pulled into the parking lot between the Physical Activity Center and the maintenance shop on A. C. Lavendar Drive, Stone knew that he was approaching the Point of No Return. Up till now, he justified, all he had done was try and think of ways to save his precious little girl. He had not done anything wrong yet. All of that was about to change when he walked in the maintenance shop. He knew everyone was there waiting on him.

If it had not been his turn to buy the tickets, he would be there waiting on whoever had bought the tickets, praying that the good life was just six numbers away.

His plan to handle the lottery group, guys he considered to be his best friends, was simple. Luckily, the set of winning numbers had been on the ticket that had the single number on it. At quick glance, all Mega Millions lottery tickets looked the same, except for the date they had printed on them.

Stone was going to walk into the maintenance shop, looking all dejected, and pretend they had not won. He was going to throw the tickets on the table and say "Take a look boys; we won a total of $15 on these tickets. One number and the Mega Millions ball. Some lucky son of a bitch took all your money."

Stone would be careful with what he said. He did not want to lie. The tickets that he threw on the table had won $15 and the lucky son of a bitch that took their money was Stone.

He was certainly leaving out information, yes, but was not technically lying.

Technically was a word you used when you knew you were wrong, but were grabbing at straws to make your case.

Stone's biggest fear at the moment was Carter King. He was a detail man. If he looked closely at the tickets, he might notice that the single ticket was actually for the next Mega Millions drawing on Friday. If Stone could get by Carter, the ruse was on. If Carter noticed the date on the new ticket, Stone would act surprised and wonder what could have happened to the missing group ticket. He would "think" and then remember that he had dropped the tickets when he was getting back into the car after buying them because he was in a hurry. Then they would all go out to his car and find the ticket between the seat and the console where he had strategically placed it a few minutes ago. Then, hopefully, the group would be so happy that they were millionaires that they wouldn't notice how Stone had just tried to steal their money.

*****

It was 8:04 am when Stone punched the time clock. He was four minutes late. The room was full. Every one of the lottery group members was there. Stone saw Carter sitting in the back of the room near the coffee pot. He made eye contact, but quickly broke it off.

The questions started immediately as Stone walked in. "Tell us we are millionaires!" shouted Mark Sloan. He was the hyper one of the bunch.

"Yea, tell us we can call City Hall and tell them to take this job and shove it where the sun don't shine," added Will Wall. Will did not like anything about the city or his job except his weekly paycheck.

Stone threw the tickets on the table. "Take a look boys; we won a total of $15 on these tickets. One number and the Mega Millions ball. Some lucky son of a bitch took your money," he told them just like he had rehearsed. It sounded good, believable.

Pee Wee Cooper grabbed up the tickets and looked through them, obviously hoping Stone was playing a joke on them. Little did Pee Wee know how close he was to the truth.

Stone continued to keep things focused on him rather than the tickets. "I can't believe somebody bought the winning ticket at the same store we buy our tickets at. I wonder if we will know 'em."

"Of course we will know them," said Justin Turner. "We know just about everybody that goes to the Corner Grocery. I just hope I'm kin to them." Justin had lived in Roswell all his life. His family had moved to Roswell in 1902 when it was nothing more than a crossroads. Nowadays, Roswell was the 7th largest city in Georgia with a population topping 100,000.

"I hope they are a friend of mine," Will Wall re-joined into the discussion. "I know if I won that kind of money, I would share with my friends."

"You are so full of shit Will that I am surprised you don't get flushed on a regular basis." This comment came from Pee Wee. He thought he was Mr. Wit. Most people thought of him as Mr. Witless.

"I told y'all we wouldn't win anything. I don't know why we even keep playing. All we are doing is throwing money down the drain," said Bart Henderson, always the skeptic. "I don't think I am going to play anymore."

Everyone was watching Pee Wee go through the tickets, looking for the golden egg. Stone was getting nervous. Too many eyes saw too much. He just hoped Carter did not get involved in the ticket review project that was unfolding.

Just as Carter got up, Bart Henderson, their supervisor, spoke up, "Well, that water leak ain't going to fix itself. Let's get going. Today's assignments are posted on my door like they always are. Carter, why don't you and Pee Wee go warm up the trucks? It's colder than a witch's titty in a brass bra out there. Y'all be careful today and stay warm."

As they were leaving the break room Carter turned and looked Stone straight in the eye and said, "You sure we didn't win the money and you're just trying to stiff us?"

Stone's heart stopped beating for what seemed like hours. He managed to hold Carter's stare and reply, "I wish. If that was true all my problems would be solved and I wouldn't be getting ready to get into a big wet hole, now would I?"

Carter looked at him funny, winked, and then just walked off.

That went well, thought Stone. *This might just work.*

*****

The day dragged on. The wind was cold and uninviting. The hole that held the 6-inch water line that had broken was just downright miserable. On top of that, the temperature did not go up as the day went on. It just got colder and wetter outside.

To be Georgia's newest multi-millionaire, Stone Lee was having a bad day. Twice Stone had let the wrench slip he was working with and had busted his knuckles.

Justin noticed. "Stone, I've never seen you bust your knuckles before, much less twice in one day. You must have something else on your mind. Don't tell me that little waitress at Hooters has your mind wandering? What was her name?"

"Margaret," offered Pee Wee.

"Yea, Margaret," Justin continued. "Last time we ate there she couldn't get you enough sweet tea."

"Lay off me, will ya?" Stone groaned. "My hands are cold and wet, my feet are colder and wetter and my back hurts. Margaret doesn't even know I'm alive and even if she did, I'm not going Chipper Jones on her." Chipper Jones was an Atlanta Braves icon. He made the tabloids when his marriage broke up over his alleged relationship with a Hooters waitress.

"OK," Justin said. "But you should be wearing gloves anyway. You know the rules." The City of Roswell had policies in place that required workers to wear gloves, protective eyewear and ear plugs when they used certain equipment and worked in certain situations. Working in a big, wet, deep hole was certainly one of those situations.

*****

Lunch time found most of the lottery group eating sandwiches in the maintenance shop and watching TV. In warmer times, they almost always went somewhere to eat lunch. They had regular spots like Rhea's hamburger joint, Hooters, and Slope's BBQ, but with the temperature hanging around 32 degrees, nobody wanted to go anywhere.

The 12 noon local news was on. Most of the guys liked to watch CBS Channel 46 because of the new weather personality, Dagmar Metcalf. Dagmar had arrived on the weather scene a few months earlier and had taken the town by storm, so to speak.

Dagmar was well endowed and often gave viewers a glimpse of cleavage. So why not enjoy watching the weather woman while getting the weather? All the stations reported the same stuff. Stone had even heard rumors that some folks around town planned their day around Dagmar's weather forecast.

"The Siberian Express has locked its sights on the Deep South and it will arrive sometime late Thursday night or early Friday morning," Dagmar said. "Depending on the timing of the arrival of the moisture from the Gulf of Mexico, we could be in for up to 3 inches of wintery mix. If the cold weather arrives before the moisture, we could have 3-4 inches of snow. If the moisture arrives first, we could see a couple of inches of rain that will freeze where it hits. Stay tuned to Channel 46. We will track the storm for you and let you know what to expect."

"I sure hope she is wrong about the snow," said Mark Sloan. "I hate it when we have to work in the snow and ice."

"Maybe it will snow enough to shut down the whole town," said Will Wall. "It would be nice to get a day off with the kids and the snow."

"I don't know what I am going to do if they close schools down," said Stone. "I don't have any sick leave or vacation days left and I have nobody to leave the kids with."

Stone had not told his co-workers about the extent of Paula's deteriorating condition. He had taken a lot of days off with her but that was not unusual. Most of the lottery group used sick leave like vacation days. As soon as they had accrued time they took it whether they were sick or not. City policy allows employees two sick days in a row without a doctor's note.

"How's your daughter doing, Stone?" asked Carter. "She's been sick a lot lately, hasn't she?"

The question caught Stone off guard. "She had the flu, but seems to be getting better."

Stone could feel the noose tighten around his neck. He would put a plan together and put it into effect as soon as possible. He and Paula were running out of time.

*****

Quitting time finally arrived and not soon enough for Stone. He was the first to hit the time clock and he almost ran to his car. He needed to think.

As he hurried out, he noticed Carter King was sitting at the table with the lottery tickets in front of him. Carter looked at him, glanced down at the tickets, looked back up and winked.

What did that mean? Stone thought. *Nothing.* He tried to shake it off. *Carter is a winker. Don't get paranoid.*

Just stick to the plan. He had, as close as he could figure, $125,000,000 just waiting to be claimed. That was enough to save his daughter's life and a lot more.

But he couldn't forget that he had lied to his co-workers and friends. They trusted him and he let them down. Guilt began creeping into Stone's conscience.

Maybe he should just come clean with them and tell them the truth. Explain to them what had happened and how he was just trying to save his daughter's life. Tell them he needed more money than his share to keep her alive. Surely they would give him and Paula what they needed.

But what if they didn't? What if they were all selfish bastards and laughed at him and his problems?

Stone also knew that there were many variables when it came to the medical procedure Paula needed. What if things got complicated in Mexico and other expenses popped up?

What if she needed extra medical attention once they got back home?

He could not, for Paula's sake, take that chance. He had to do whatever he had to do to take care of his daughter. He had promised Kathy. He had to make sure his daughter got what she needed and that Steven was taken care of during this time as well.

No, Stone thought. *I'm not giving anything away until I know my family is taken care of.*

Stone, do whatever it takes to take care of our kids.

Chapter 6

Wednesday

Stone was driving down tree-lined Canton Street. He usually enjoyed this part of the drive from the Roswell Area Park to Waller Park to pick up his kids.

Canton Street had made a great comeback in the last couple of years. There were many restaurants and gift shops that were now doing a brisk business, even in the cold weather.

Kathy's favorite shop had been The Chandlery. This unique gift shop had many unusual and beautiful items and was located in the heart of the Canton Street shopping district. Kathy could always find just the right gift for anyone there.

The Lee family's favorite place to eat in downtown Roswell was Diesel's. The old gas station turned pizza pub was actually on Highway 9 and not Canton Street, but was still part of Historic Roswell.

Diesel's featured an SOP (Sausage, onion & pepper) sandwich, which was Stone's favorite. The kids, of course, liked the pizza.

Neither shopping nor food was on Stone's radar right now. All he could focus on was his plan. He had to turn in the ticket, get the money, and save his daughter. Then he would split up what was left and give it to the lottery group.

He had to do all of this without anyone knowing what was going on. Not an easy plan. But he had no choice. He had to save his daughter.

*****

As he pulled into Waller Park Recreation Center, he saw Eli Baker.

Timing...the key to life.

He had known Eli most of his life. They had gone to Roswell North Elementary School, Crabapple Middle School and Roswell High School together. At Roswell High they played football together. When they were seniors, they even doubled dated to the Prom. After the Prom, Eli should have been arrested for DUI, but because of Stone's quick thinking, Eli had dodged certain jail time. Eli had promised Stone that he would make it up to him one day. After that incident, however, Stone and Eli had drifted apart.

Eli had changed over the last couple of years. His daughter was the same age as Paula, so Stone and Eli often crossed paths, but the friendship was just not there. Eli now gave Stone the willies. Stone could not put his finger on it, but it always seemed that Eli was looking over his shoulder, as though someone was trying to sneak up on him.

Stone wished he could have circled the block and come back when Eli was gone. But, as usual, he was in a hurry. Paula had a drawing class at the Visual Arts Center and then it was off to Midweek at Roswell United Methodist Church.

According to the kids, RUMC was the coolest of the churches in Roswell. They had built a youth center called the Dodd, named after the retired pastor, Malone Dodson. The Dodd was a safe haven for the kids of Roswell. They could play, hang out, have fun and get a little gospel training while they were there. Stone made sure Paula and Steven attended Midweek as often as they could.

"Hey Stone," Eli called, "Cold enough for you?"

"I'm ready for summer," replied Stone. "I don't much like the cold weather."

"Me neither. Hey, did you hear who won the lottery? It almost has to be someone we know." Eli was a regular at the Corner Grocery.

"Last I heard," Stone said, "nobody had claimed the prize yet."

"If I had won," Eli began, "I would get my act together before I came forward to claim my money. You know, get an accountant, a body guard, a tax guy and a banker. That way I'd be insulated from the media. It would be crazy."

If there was one thing Stone did not want to do, it was to get into another lottery discussion, especially with Eli. He decided he would change the direction of the conversation.

"You selling any cars these days?" Stone asked. Eli was a used car salesman. He worked at one of the many used car lots on Highway 9 in Roswell. The place he worked advertised "classic cars for less." Of course, the cars were anything but classics. While they had many high-end type cars on the lot, most of them had a questionable past. Eli had told him once that you can't always trust a Car Fax.

"Not doing that anymore," Eli answered. "The owner and I had a little disagreement about commission percentages. I lost the argument and my job."

"That's too bad. Times are tough," was all Stone could think to say.

"Not to worry," Eli the optimist said. "Something will come up. Keep me in mind if you hear or think of anything. Right now I would do almost anything to make a few bucks. Mama's house payment is due in a week and we ain't got the money yet." He leaned in close to Stone and added in a whisper, "And that ain't my biggest problem." Then he returned to his regular voice and said, "I just got to stay positive. Something will happen."

You might just be right, thought Stone. The details of the next step in his plan were coming together.

Chapter 7

Wednesday

Usually, after the kids went to bed, Stone sat at the kitchen table looking over the many bills he had to pay, but not tonight. He spent this night perfecting his plan which was actually rather simple. So simple it might just work.

He would ask Eli if he wanted to make $1,000,000 cash. All Eli would have to do is turn in the winning ticket, smile for the cameras, collect the money, keep $1,000,00, give the rest to Stone, and, this was the biggie, keep his mouth shut.

Eli would get enough money to pay his mortgage and take care of his other problem, whatever it was. Stone would get enough money to get his daughter the medical attention and procedures she needed, take care of all expenses while they were in Mexico, and allow for Steven to remain in Roswell while Stone and Paula were in Mexico so his life would not be interrupted. Then, when Paula was taken care of, Stone would distribute the remaining money to his lottery group based on their original shares. Everybody wins.

Stone's biggest concern was Eli. Could he be trusted to keep the secret? Could he be trusted to give Stone the money once he turned in the ticket? Maybe he should offer Eli more than $1,000,000. Maybe $5,000,000 would be a better incentive to keep Stone's secret. He needed to make sure it was enough to make it worth Eli's effort, enough money to keep Eli quiet and happy. But Stone did not want to give Eli too much money because he really wanted to give his lottery group as much as he could once Paula was taken care of. After all, it was their money.

*****

The lead story on WSB Channel 2's 11:00 pm news was still the lottery ticket. It had not yet been turned in and everyone was wondering why. The reporter was standing outside the Corner Grocery. It was closed, but for some reason local television stations thought that it was more compelling to be on site for a story, even if the site was locked up and no one was around.

There was no real news to report. The ticket had been sold, but not yet turned in. The reporter had already interviewed a couple of Roswell residents and the store owner earlier that week. While the identity of the person who had bought the ticket was still not known, the cheerful reporter was hopeful that the individual would come forward soon. The news team at Channel 2 promised to follow this developing story closely until the winner was found.

Stone started drifting off during the lottery story. As he fell asleep, he was trying to figure out exactly what to say to Eli and how to ensure that Eli would give him the money once he cashed the ticket in. Of course, Eli owed him and they had been good friends once, so surely he could be trusted. However, the lottery group consisted of Stone's good friends and they thought they could trust him. Stone's last thought before he fell asleep was that Eli needed to be more trustworthy than he was.

If Stone had stayed awake a few more minutes, he might have gotten a heads up from another story on the Channel 2 nightly newscast:

BREAKING NEWS OUT OF ROSWELL.

"The Georgia Bureau of Investigation is looking into a gambling ring that has ties to Roswell. Several arrests in Atlanta have been made, with more to come in the next two weeks. The GBI indicated that the ring has ties to several metro cities including Roswell, Alpharetta and Peachtree City."

Chapter 8

Thursday

Barrett had followed Eli to the Krispy Kreme Donut Shop at the corner of Highway 9 and Oak Street. Eli did not see Barrett until he had gotten out of his car. Then it was too late.

"Where's my money, Eli?" Barrett asked. Barrett was the only name he used, like Prince or Cher. But that is where the similarities ended. Barrett was big, mean and all business. Barrett had been around a long time. Despite that fact, very little was known about him, except everybody knew you did not mess with Barrett. Obviously, Eli had forgotten that important point.

"I need a couple of days," Eli said without much conviction. "I'll get it."

"Why should I give you any more time? You owe me money. I'm here to collect it or make adjustments to your body."

Eli was sweating. "Look Barrett, if you hurt me now, you won't get your money. If you give me a little time, I will get you the money. If I don't, you can hurt me twice as much later. How's that for a plan?"

Barrett thought for a minute, and then broke into a big smile. "I tell you what I am going to do. You got one week. Seven days. 168 hours. 10,080 minutes. Then your time's up. You will pay one way or the other. Am I making myself clear here?" Barrett asked.

Eli was impressed with Barrett's math skills. Under different circumstances he would have told him so.

Barrett continued, "Have I mentioned the interest penalty that starts today?" Barrett waited for Eli to reply. He was in no hurry.

Eli finally realized that an answer was expected. "No, I didn't know there would be an interest penalty."

"$10,000 for every day you don't pay, starting now." Barrett explained. "So adding today's interest penalty, you owe me $760,000. And just in case you are thinking about being a smart ass, no, I don't take checks or American Express.

Being a smart ass had not occurred to Eli. He was just trying to get through this with all his teeth still in his mouth. "I'm working a deal. I'll have the money by the end of the week."

"Eli, keep your mouth shut, OK? You make those promises you know you ain't going to keep. Just get my money by this time next week and you and your family can live life to the fullest. Don't pay and things will change. Do you understand me, Eli? Life ain't always a tea party."

Barrett's voice had taken on a new tone. It was cold, calculating, and it sent chills down Eli's spine.

Eli had made some really bad decisions in his life. He was always the first one to get into trouble and the last to get out. A few years ago he had turned his life around because of his daughter Brenda. He realized that he was missing out on the most important part of his life. So he gave up the booze, the drugs, the gambling and the women and started trying to do the right thing. It was tougher than he thought. All the jobs he got were minimum wage types. But he had made a commitment to Brenda and he saw it through. Things were going well until about 10 months ago.

He was hanging out at the local bowling alley with some friends on a regular Saturday afternoon. A friend of a friend was talking about how he had made a killing the week before, betting on football games. He let it be known that if anyone wanted any action that he had a connection. Eli had just sold two "classic cars" and had a few extra dollars.

Although he knew he shouldn't, he asked the guy to set him up with some action.

Eli got what he asked for. He won a few thousand dollars the first two weeks, but then his life started spinning out of control. He lost $2,500 in one bet, and then tried to make it up on the next one. Before he knew it, he was $10,000 in the hole. Then the harder he tried to get out, the deeper he got. He kept saying, "My luck has got to change."

And it did; it went from bad to worse.

Now he found himself $760,000 in debt with absolutely no way to pay. He wanted to run, but he knew he couldn't. If he ran, then Barrett would go after Brenda.

He had 7 days to figure things out. If push came to shove, he would have to send Brenda off. Brenda would not want to go. He would have to get his half-sister, Mandy, who lived in Marion, South Carolina, involved.

Marion, South Carolina was a sleepy little town near Myrtle Beach. Nobody would think to look there for anybody. Mandy would take care of Brenda. Nobody knew about Mandy and she would be hard to find since their last names were not the same. Mandy was the offspring of one of his father's many field trips around the southeast.

"I understand you, Barrett," Eli finally said. "I'll get you the money, one way or the other."

"That's what I wanted to hear. Just so you understand, for the next seven days I will know where you are all the time. Don't think you can outsmart me, outrun me or out maneuver me. I already know all your options. Just get the money."

There was no doubt that Barrett knew what he was talking about.

Eli had seven days to save his little girl. He needed a miracle to get out of this.

Chapter 9

Thursday

Stone just wanted to get through the day. The lottery craze was waning a little. As he turned by the Corner Grocery, he saw that there were no news crews on the scene. The Atlanta Journal Constitution had reduced the story about the newest Georgia Millionaire to the third page of the Metro Section. The unclaimed lottery ticket was fading fast in most folks' minds. Stone hoped the same would be true when he got to work.

The kids didn't like it much, but they had left the house early today. Stone was hoping to be one of the first to get to the maintenance shop. He had even skipped reading the newspaper this morning. If he could get there soon enough, he was hoping to grab the lottery tickets and dispose of them. The single ticket purchased on the day after the winning lottery drawing was the only true connection to what he was doing.

Pee Wee was always the first person in each and every morning. He seemed to know when anyone was coming in early and just got there before them. He would unlock the doors, turn up the heat and get the coffee brewing. No one knew why he came in so early, he just did. Of course, no one objected to having the heat turned on and the coffee made when they got there. Everyone appreciated it, though no one ever said anything.

Stone shook his head when he pulled into the parking lot at 7:26 am. Pee Wee's Silverado pick-up truck was there in its usual spot, and so was Carter's Jeep Wrangler.

Stone could not believe his bad luck. Carter was almost always late getting to work. He was never there early. In fact, Bart had written Carter up with an employee warning report just last month. After the report, Carter was not late, but he was never more than 4 or 5 minutes early. So why, on this day, was Carter already here? Stone was getting a bad feeling in the pit of his stomach.

He told himself, *don't panic and don't get paranoid.*

*****

When Stone walked into the break room, Pee Wee and Carter were sitting, drinking coffee and watching "Good Morning Atlanta" on Channel 5. Stone could not help but glance first at the table and look for the tickets. On the table was this week's edition of the *Roswell Neighbor*, one of three local newspapers. The Roswell Neighbor came out every Wednesday. It carried all the regular local news like politics, what was happening in the Rotary Club and, of course, the DUIs and drug arrests for the week. Unlike a few years ago, most of the DUIs and the drug arrests these days consisted of people who were not from Roswell and whose names very few Roswell natives could pronounce. Right next to the *Neighbor* was Thursday's edition of the Atlanta Journal Constitution.

When Stone looked up from the table, Carter was staring at him. He winked. Stone had no idea why. His nerves were standing on end.

While Stone wanted to grab the newspaper and throw it aside to see if the tickets were still on the table, he fought the impulse. He walked slowly over to the coffee pot and poured himself a cup. As casually as he could, he glanced into the only trash can in the break room. It was completely empty. No tickets.

When Stone turned around, Carter was still looking at him. Stone ignored the stare and did his best to pretend that it did not bother him. Maybe Carter had just figured out how good looking Stone was. This thought made Stone smile ever so slightly. He sat down right next to Carter.

Keep your friends close and your enemies closer.

He sat his coffee cup down and reached for the newspaper. As usual, the sports section of the AJC was on top.

The sports headlines read:

"Clemson Upsets UNC"

Stone's team, the Clemson University Tigers, had beaten one of the perennial powerhouses of the Atlantic Coast Conference by a score of 89-88. He had been so focused on his plan last night that he completely forgot the game was on ESPN. From the looks at the score, he had missed a great game.

Stone decided to play it cool. "Great game last night, huh? I can't believe my Tigers didn't blow it like they usually do."

Carter was still looking at him. Without breaking his gaze, he asked, "What did you think about that call the official made with two seconds left in the game?"

Stone was stuck. He had no idea what had happened or what Carter was talking about. Carter was waiting, staring.

Pee Wee rescued him. "I think it was a sack of shit. Who calls a technical with two seconds left in a game?"

The University of North Carolina Tar Heels were winning 88-87 when UNC's big man missed a shot in the paint. The UNC coach and all the folks dressed in Carolina blue thought he had been fouled. All three referees and all the folks dressed in Clemson orange disagreed. Clemson got the rebound and quickly called a time out.

As the teams were heading for their benches, the UNC coach began his assault on the officials. His face was red and his temples were bulging. He was yelling at the nearest official and kept moving closer and closer to him. By the time the second official came over to help calm the situation down, the coach was close to the big tiger paw that sits in the middle of the floor at Clemson's Littlejohn Coliseum. The second official was unsuccessful in calming the coach. In fact, the situation got worse. The UNC coach started to yell at both of the officials and then did the unthinkable. He poked the second official in the chest with his pointer finger.

It was automatic at that point. Both officials simultaneously placed their right hand perpendicularly to their left hand in the sign of a "T". The technical foul gave the Tigers two free throws and they made both shots. They also got the ball and, following a quick throw-in, the game was over. The two second technical would be replayed and reviewed almost constantly on Sports Center for the next 24 hours.

Carter was still looking at Stone.

Stone returned his gaze and said, "It's about time one went our way. We don't usually get those kinds of calls."

Stone put down the Sports Section and dug for the front page from the bottom of the stack. When he pulled it out, he did it in such a way that he could see what was under all the papers.

Nothing. No tickets. Where were the tickets? They were not on the table and not in the trash can.

Why didn't he just wait around yesterday and pick them up after everyone had left? Now there was evidence of his lie and his attempt to steal $125,000,000.

*****

Right after lunch, Stone got a call from the clinic at Roswell North Elementary School. The school literally sat right next to the Roswell Area Park. The school and the park had a joint use agreement which allowed facilities to be shared by both groups. The proximity of the school to the park allowed Stone to respond quickly when Paula needed him.

Paula was at the clinic, complaining about stomach cramps. That was not good. The doctors had warned Stone that her body would start reacting harshly to the kidney disease, but they had said the cramps and pain were probably 6-9 months away. Once the cramps started, however, the countdown of how long Paula could live without a new kidney would be less than 30 days.

Stone was at the lake in Roswell Area Park, clearing goose poop from the gravel trail, when he got the call. He took the short cut to the school, which took him down by the tennis complex, along the lighted walking path, down the outfield of Field #2, over the bridge and by Field #1. This was one of the small fields where the 7 and 8-year-olds played baseball. Stone couldn't help but remember how much fun it was to watch Steven play baseball on this field when he was 7 and was more worried about whether his hat had the right bend in the brim than how to catch a fly ball.

He entered the school through the front door and waved at Ms. Christy at the front desk. Usually, visitors were supposed to sign in and get a visitor's badge, but everyone at the school knew Stone. They knew where he was heading, too. Paula was sick again.

As Stone entered the clinic, he saw Paula on the small cot. She had a cold cloth on her forehead.

"She's much better now. She was in a good bit of pain a few minutes ago," whispered Janet Mullins, the school nurse. Janet volunteered in the school's clinic three days a week. She had two kids at Roswell North. Her son, Colby, was a third grader. Her daughter, Jade, was in kindergarten. Janet's husband had died in a plane accident several years earlier.

Janet and Stone had dated a couple of times. They had hit it off well, but it was hard for them to find time to see each other. She knew the complete story about Paula.

"Thanks," was all Stone could think to say. Their eyes held a quick gaze that, under any other circumstances, Stone would have enjoyed.

He leaned down and touched Paula's hand. She immediately opened her eyes and her face registered relief at the sight of her dad.

"Hey baby. How are you doing?"

"I'm OK, Daddy. My stomach's not hurting anymore. Don't make me go home. I want to stay at school."

"Baby, I think we should go to the doctor."

"I don't want to, Daddy. I want to stay at school. We have Fireman Brandon coming to visit with us this afternoon."

Fireman Brandon was a favorite among the elementary school children. He came and showed the kids the entire fireman's suit. He even let them try on his helmet.

Stone looked up at Janet. She placed an understanding hand on his shoulder and offered a warm smile.

He kissed Paula on the cheek and said, "I'm going to call Dr. Ishmael and see what he has to say." Stone stood up and stepped out into the hallway to make the call.

Stone had Dr. Ishmael's number on speed dial. The doctor picked up on the second ring. Dr. Ishmael recognized Stone's number.

Stone quickly went through what had happened. Dr. Ishmael took a deep breath. He had promised Stone that he would always be up front and brutally honest.

"This is not good. The cramps will come and go at first. They have arrived much earlier than we had anticipated. Usually, once they start, there is 5 to 6 hours between them.

You can tell how quickly the kidney is shutting down by the length of time between cramps."

"Is there anything I can do?" asked Stone, although he already knew the answer.

"No," Doctor Ishmael answered. "Our only hope now is Mexico."

Stone ignored the last remark. "Can I leave her at school today?"

"If she wants to stay, I see no reason not to let her."

"Thanks Doctor."

Stone walked back into the clinic. Paula was sitting up now, looking much better. "Are you sure you want to stay?"

"Yes Daddy. This might be my only chance to meet Fireman Brandon." This brought tears to both Stone's and Janet's eyes.

Stone stood and picked Paula up and gave her a bear hug. "OK, go see Fireman Brandon. When you see him, ask him about the Easter Bunny." Fireman Brandon had stepped in at the last minute at the city's egg hunt when the real bunny girl did not show up.

Paula looked at her dad like he was crazy, but said, "OK Daddy, I will. Thanks, Ms. Mullins."

Stone awkwardly gave Janet a hug. "Thanks." He had more he wanted to say, but he knew the timing was not right.

As Stone followed Paula out of the clinic, he realized that he had to put the plan into action today.

Chapter 10

Thursday

Every time Stone went to pick up Steven and Paula at Waller Park Recreation Center at 5:30 pm, Eli had been there, too. Stone hoped that Eli would continue to be a creature of habit today.

As Stone pulled the Trooper into the parking lot, he saw his luck was holding. Eli's old grey Ford Crown Victoria was parked in the handicap spot closest to the building. Eli had gotten the handicap placard that hung from his rear view mirror almost two years ago when he had knee surgery. He had blown out his knee playing co-ed softball. The placard had long ago expired, but he kept putting tape over the date and writing in new dates. So far, he had not been caught.

As Stone walked into the recreation center, Eli was leaning against the entrance wall. Stone approached Eli.

"What's happening?" Eli asked as Stone got close.

"Not much," Stone answered.

"Think it's gonna snow?" Eli asked.

"I hope not," Stone replied. "Snow days are rough. We have to work all day in that wet, cold stuff, clearing ice and throwing sand. And the whole time I wonder why folks don't just stay home. I don't know what happens in yoga class, but it can't be that important."

"Quit ya bitching, Stone. At least you got a job. Got money coming in regularly. Look at me. Unemployed, broke and over my head in debt," Eli said to Stone. Eli was talking to Stone, but the whole time he was looking out the window. Watching.

Stone moved a little closer to Eli and said, "I think I can help."

"What did ya say?" Eli asked, looking Stone in the eye for the first time.

"I think I can help with your financial situation," Stone repeated.

"I'm listening," Eli said and Stone could tell that he really was.

"We can't talk here," again Stone was whispering.

"Why not?" Eli asked.

"You'll understand when I tell you," Stone said mysteriously. "Can you meet me later tonight?"

Now it was Stone's turn to look around. Secrecy was paramount.

"I guess. When and where?" Eli was obviously getting annoyed by the lack of information, but he just as obviously needed money.

"Let's meet tonight at 8 pm at the 1000 Hills Coffee Shop up there on Highway 9, next to the 2nd Baptist Church." Stone offered.

"I know the place. You sure this is going to be worth my time?" Eli asked.

Stone smiled and said, "Oh yeah. And then some."

Chapter 11

Thursday

The 1000 Hills Coffee Shop was locally owned and operated. Jonathan Golden had opened the shop a couple of years ago. The shop's motto was: **Drink Coffee – Do Good**.

The **Drink Coffee** part was easy to figure out. They sold coffee by the cup or by the bag. They also had pastries and other good stuff.

The **Do Good** part represented the efforts to improve the daily lives of the coffee growers in Rwanda. The 1000 Hills Coffee Shop purchased their coffee beans directly from the farmers and paid a higher than average rate for the coffee beans. This allowed the Rwandan farmers the opportunity to improve their lives, their families and their communities. **Drink Coffee, Do Good.**

Stone arrived before Eli. He ordered a hot chocolate. While the coffee was good, the hot chocolate was exceptional. It was not only tasty; 1000 Hills made it look pretty, too.

Eli arrived right on time and ordered an espresso from Adria who was working the counter.

Even before he could sit down, Eli was demanding, "OK, tell me how you are going to help me with my financial situation."

Stone took a deep breath and went through the whole story. He did not leave anything out. He told Eli about his daughter's illness and how she needed expensive medical procedures. He explained about the lottery group, the tickets and the winning numbers. He explained his plan about Eli turning in the ticket for him, smiling for the cameras, paying the taxes, keeping $1,000,000 in cash and then giving Stone the rest.

When he was finished, Eli just stared at him.

Finally, Eli cocked his head, smiled and said a lot louder than Stone liked, "Man, I can't believe you would drag me out at night to go and make up a pile of shit like that!"

Stone looked around and then leaned over the table and said, "Keep your voice down. I thought you would react like that. Look at this." Stone handed him the winning lottery ticket.

Eli studied the ticket. "How do I know this ain't just another losing ticket?"

Stone was ready for this question. He reached in his pocket and pulled out the daily lottery printout for Tuesday. The printout listed all the winning numbers for all lottery games played on Tuesday, including the Mega Millions.

Eli held up both tickets. His eyes kept darting from the ticket to the printout. Stone could read his lips as he compared the numbers. "2-12-15-27-29-2" After the third time he mouthed the numbers, it hit him.

"Oh my god! This is the winning ticket!" Eli said in a voice so high it sounded like somebody else was talking. "Are you sure you ain't screwing with me?"

Stone was again leaning over the table, still whispering, "I ain't screwing with you, but you got to keep your voice down. Nobody can know that I got the ticket."

With that, Stone reached across the table and grabbed the ticket out of Eli's hand. The situation had hit Eli hard. He was trying to clear his head and wrap his mind around the circumstances at hand.

Stone continued. "Look Eli, I know this is a lot to throw at you, but I don't have much time. Are you in or not?"

"Of course I'm in." What else was Eli going to say?

Stone knew that this was the most critical point in their new partnership. He had to be able to trust Eli. Once he turned over the ticket to Eli, Stone could lose everything. Eli could take the ticket, turn it in, and collect the money and then just walk away. Who would believe anyone would give someone else the winning ticket to turn in? It just didn't make sense. No one would trust someone like Eli with $125,000,000 and hope for the best.

"Listen Eli, here's the deal. I need to know I can trust you. You've got to hand over the money after you get it, minus your take. Can you do that? Can I trust you?"

Stone did not know how to take the pause before Eli's response. Was Eli thinking about whether he was going to run when he got the cash, or was he trying to decide if he could be trusted? Either way, Stone did not like the fact that Eli had to think about it.

Finally, Eli looked him dead in the eye and said, "I don't know why you picked me, but the more I think about it, the less I really care. All I know is that this deal came along at just the right time for me."

Timing... the key to life.

Eli continued, "I'll do it, but I think my time and effort is worth a little more than $1,000,000. I think I'm worth $5,000,000.

OK, Stone thought, *here we go. The negotiation phase of the partnership.*

"Look Eli, this ain't my money. I just want to save my daughter's life and then give as much money as I can to my friends who deserve it. $1,000,000 is a lot for what I am asking you to do. Otherwise, you are out of the deal and get zero." Stone delivered this just as he had practiced.

Eli's eyes turned cold as ice. Now it was his turn to lean across the table and whisper. "There ain't no way in hell you are closing me out of this deal. Remember, I know all the guys that you owe millions to. And don't think I would hesitate for even a second to tell them. I'm going to turn the ticket in and get my $5,000,000 or I'm going to call the boys at the park and the TV folks, too. Then you go to prison and your daughter dies."

So far, Eli was responding exactly as Stone thought he would. Stone took a deep breath for effect. Now both men were leaning across the table. Their noses were mere inches apart. "Look, let's not start our partnership off on the wrong foot. This will work for both of us. I get to save Paula and you get a nice bankroll. Remember, Eli, you owe me."

At this comment, Eli settled back into his chair. Had it not been for Stone, Eli would have been sent to prison for at least a year.

It all happened the night of the Senior Prom. The Prom was being held at the Fox Theater in downtown Atlanta. Stone and Eli had agreed to double date. Eli's Ford Crown Victoria had plenty of room in the front seat and back seat.

During the Prom, Eli had too many shots of Wild Turkey, a bottle of which he had hidden in his tuxedo. When it was time to leave, Stone begged Eli to let him drive, but Eli convinced Stone that he'd had only one drink.

Ten minutes into the trip back to Roswell on Georgia 400, an Atlanta policeman was behind them with his blue lights flashing. Eli was going crazy. He was saying that he knew he would blow positive for DUI and that this would be his third, and since he had just turned 18, he would fall victim to the "three strikes and you are out" law in Georgia. Basically, when convicted of DUI for the third time an automatic year in prison was the required punishment.

Just as the policeman was walking up to Eli's car, another motorist blew his horn and came within inches of hitting the officer. The policeman jumped onto the trunk of Eli's car and rolled down behind it. This move saved the cop's life. It also provided the opening that Stone used to save Eli.

Timing... the key to life.

Stone took advantage of the confusion and literally dragged Eli from the front seat into the back seat. Just as quickly, he bolted into the front seat. When the policeman finally got up, gathered himself, and came up to the window, Stone was able to convince the policeman that he had not been drinking and that he had swerved a little when he dropped the CD that he was trying to get into the CD player.

Both Eli and Stone remembered Eli's words on that fateful night. "I'll repay you someday, Stone. I will make it up to you. All you got to do is ask."

Now, in the coffee shop, Stone's facial expression softened and he said in as non-threatening a manner as he could, "You owe me, Eli. I'm asking you to return the favor."

*****

Stone left the 1000 Hills Coffee Shop before Eli. They agreed they would meet on Friday at 1:00 pm and go to the Georgia Lottery office together. Eli would turn in the ticket, but Stone would be driving. They figured that Friday afternoon would be the best time because it would be hard for the media to get the story on the 6:00 pm news. Plus, Eli could lay low on Saturday and Sunday, and hope by Monday things would have died down enough that they could go to the bank and get their financial matters in order.

Eli agreed to help for a negotiated fee of $3,000,000. Stone felt good about the meeting. He had been prepared to go to $4,000,000, so he felt he had won. With all that was going on, he thought nothing of Eli's request to borrow $50 to pay his babysitter. Stone forgot that Eli and his daughter lived with Eli's mother.

As Stone turned left onto Highway 9, sleet had just begun to fall. He looked back to see Eli still sitting at the front table. Stone had not seen that look in Eli's eyes since Prom night.

What Stone did not see was Carter sitting in the church parking lot beside the coffee shop, watching.

Chapter 12

Friday

Stone had hit the snooze button on the alarm. He almost never did that. But after a restless night, he just wanted a couple of minutes more in the warm bed.

When he looked at the clock it was 7:05 am. He jumped up and immediately woke up the kids. Paula was not feeling well and did not get up right away. Steven got out of bed, looked out the window and yelled, "Dad, why did you wake us up? Look outside. No way we are going to school today."

Stone had forgotten all about the weather. He looked out and saw that Steven was right. It had snowed last night. It looked like maybe an inch on the back deck.

He turned on the TV. The weather was the top story. Stone was right, a little more than an inch had fallen overnight. In Georgia, that was enough snow to basically shut down everything. Of course schools were closed, but according to Channel 2 Severe Weather, so were most businesses. They were advising people to stay indoors, at least until the transportation folks had a chance to clear the roads.

"You're right, Steven. Y'all go back to bed."

Steven slammed his bedroom door, obviously unhappy with having been woken up on a sleep-in morning.

Stone put the Folgers coffee on and went out to get his morning paper. The snow had stopped. Everything looked so peaceful, so clean and white. Stoned wondered how the newspaper guy could get the paper delivered all across the city when most folks could not even get out of their driveways.

The snow worked in Stone's favor. Stone could call into work and say he needed to stay home with the kids since school was closed. He would not have to hurry back from his trip to the Georgia Lottery office and pick up the kids this afternoon from the after school program. The snow could not have come at a better time.

Timing… the key to life.

Stone sat down at the kitchen table with his coffee and paper. He flipped through the entire paper. There was no mention of the lottery. That was good news.

When Stone finished his first cup of coffee he called Bart. Since Fulton County schools were shut down, all the park activities had been cancelled and the buildings were closed. Bart said he already heard from several of the guys and he had enough of them coming in right now. Bart told Stone to wait until noon or so to come in, that way he could stay a little later if they needed him to.

"Look, Bart," Stone said, "I need to take the whole day off. Paula's not feeling well and I really need to stay home with her."

There were a couple of seconds of silence on the phone. Finally, Bart took a deep breath and said, "You know you are out of sick leave and PTO." PTO was short for Personal Time Off. In the old days they called it vacation time. "You'll have to take it without pay."

Stone tried to sound disheartened. "I know, but I just can't leave my little girl. She had trouble at school yesterday."

Chapter 13

Friday

Stone was on his second cup of Folgers and the sports section when he heard Paula cry out. It sounded like a wild animal caught in a trap.

Stone ran down the hall and found Paula curled up in a ball on her bed, crying. "Paula what's wrong?"

Her voice was so weak; Stone had a hard time hearing her. "It hurts like it did yesterday at school, only worse."

Stone sat down on the bed and tried to hold his daughter. It was almost impossible because she had begun to thrash back and forth, trying to get the pain out of her body. She was having no luck at all.

After what seemed like hours, but was no more than 3 or 4 minutes, Paula started relaxing. She lay back on the bed, exhausted.

The commotion had woken up Steven. He was watching in disbelief from the doorway of Paula's room. He had a combination of horror and compassion on his face. Stone looked up at Steven. "Go warm up the Trooper. I'm taking Paula to the emergency room."

As Steven went outside to warm up the Trooper and get the ice off the windshield, Stone hurried to his room to change clothes.

When he returned to Paula's room, she had managed somehow to get up and put on her favorite jeans and top. Stone said, "I was going to help you get dressed."

"I'm just trying not to be such a problem," Paula announced.

Stone got Paula's big coat and hat out of the front closet. When they were ready to go, Steven was waiting at the front door with his big coat on, too.

Surprised, Stone asked, "You going? I thought you would want to stay here and get some more sleep."

Steven replied shyly, "I want to go, just in case you need my help."

Stone thought, *My little boy is growing up into a man. A concerned, caring, loving young man.*

*****

The trip to North Fulton Hospital was not a long one, but with the inch of snow in Roswell, the drive proved to be quite the ride. Stone was thankful for the 4-wheel drive on the Trooper. The snow was easy to navigate for him, but the problem was the other folks on the road. Most of the cars out were not 4-wheel drive vehicles and most drivers were not accustomed to driving in the slippery snow. Stone and the kids saw a car lose control in front of the collection center for the US Post Office.

Right after they turned left off Holcomb Bridge Road, the cramps started again. Steven was in the back seat with Paula. He tried to hold her but that didn't work. Then he tried to rub her head, but that, too, did not work. He finally looked up at Stone and said, "Hurry, Dad."

Stone picked up his speed. Thankfully, there were not as many people on this part of Highway 9. He said to both Steven and Paula, "Hang in there. We will be there in just a couple of minutes."

The cramps began to ease as they approached the Jaguar dealership at the corner of Highway 9 and Hembree Road. When they pulled into the emergency entrance at North Fulton Hospital, Paula was sitting back up in her seat, trying hard not to cry. Stone parked right at the Emergency Room entrance door and jumped out.

"Steven, pull the car around to the parking lot and then come inside," Stone said as he was helping Paula out of the vehicle. Even under these circumstances, Steven literally jumped at the chance to get behind the wheel.

Stone took Paula inside the Emergency Room. Luckily, it was a slow morning and there was no one in the waiting room. Paula sat down in one of the oversized chairs that faced the televisions. Good Morning America was on.

It only took a couple of minutes for Stone to get Paula checked in. He asked the receptionist to please call Paula's doctor and let him know Paula needed him. She said she would.

First they checked Paula's height, weight, temperature and blood pressure, after which they sent her and Stone to examination room number 3. The nurse said a doctor would be right in.

After 20 minutes, Stone was getting anxious just sitting around. He stepped outside into the hallway and asked a nurse to check and see when the doctor was going to be there. The nurse said, "Of course. Let me see what I can find out." Stone walked back into the examination room.

After about another 10 minutes, there was a knock on the door. Stone looked up, expecting the nurse to explain what was delaying the doctor. But instead, in walked Dr. Ishmael. Stone jumped up and grabbed the doctor's hand.

"Thank you for coming, Doc."

"No problem. I was already on my way to the hospital when they called. I guess it was a good time for me to be on duty."

Timing… the key to life.

The doctor turned his attention to Paula. He looked at her chart and then chatted with her like they were old friends. The doctor always made Paula feel better.

After a few minutes of prodding, checking and examining Paula, the doctor spoke softly to the nurse.

Dr. Ishmael asked Stone to step outside into the hallway for a minute. Once outside the door, the doctor said, "Stone, I don't like what is happening. We're going to run a couple of blood tests. It will probably take an hour or so to get the results back. The nurses will keep Paula comfortable. I will be back as soon as I get the results."

The tests obviously took longer than anticipated because Stone, Steven and Paula watched three full episodes of Sponge Bob Square Pants. Stone was almost relieved when the doctor knocked and entered the room. When he saw the doctor's face, however, he knew that he would rather watch more Sponge Bob than hear what he could tell would be bad news.

"Can I speak with you, Stone?" Dr. Ishmael asked as he turned back into the hallway.

He began talking as soon as the door was closed, "I'm sorry Stone, but the kidney is shutting down much more quickly than we had anticipated. Our window of opportunity to do the transplant is closing. I now think that we only have 10-14 days to get it done."

Stone turned white and felt like he was going to throw up. "What happened?" was all he could think to say.

"It's hard to say," Doctor Ishmael said. "This disease is rare in someone so young. We just don't know what to expect. All I know is that we don't have much time."

Stone knew what he had to do. He looked furtively around the hallway before asking Dr. Ishmael, "Is there somewhere we can talk?"

*****

They walked down the hall to examination room number 5.

Once inside, Stone said, "Look Doc, I need to tell you something, but you have to promise me that you will not tell anyone. Can you do that, Doc?"

"Of course. I understand the need for confidentiality."

Stone wasted no time telling the doctor that he had won the lottery. He pulled the ticket out of his pocket and handed it to Dr. Ishmael.

Then Stone said, "Doc, you can't tell anyone. My partner and I are going to turn in the ticket today, but there are extenuating circumstances. I'll have the money in a few days. Can you make the arrangements for the transplant?"

The doctor was still looking at the ticket. Without looking up, he answered, "Of course I can. When do you think you and Paula will be able to make the trip?"

Stone had not yet thought through this part of the plan. Before Stone could give him an answer, the doctor said, "I think I can get all the necessary arrangements made in about a week. I think you should be prepared to leave next Thursday or Friday. We will need to make all the financial arrangements before you leave. I know this is not much notice, but we are running out of time."

Stone had little choice. He looked the doctor in the eye and said, "Make the arrangements. I'll have the money by then and have Paula ready." The doctor shook Stone's hand and said, "I'll make the arrangements and I will call you when they are done."

"Thanks Doctor and remember, mum's the word. "

Stone walked back into the room, thinking about all that he had to do. He knew that not only did he have many things to do, but he also had to do them in the right order if he was going to save his daughter. It was going to be tough, but he was going make sure things turned out right.

Timing... the key to life.

Chapter 14

Friday

Paula, Steven and Stone finally arrived back home around 11:30 am. They had to make a couple of stops on the way back to the house. First, they stopped at the Walgreen's in Kings Plaza to pick up Paula's medicine. The doctor had written a prescription that would allow Paula to rest and hopefully keep the cramps at bay.

Their second stop was at Publix on King Road. Stone needed to pick up some groceries so the kids would have something to eat over the next day or so. Publix was Stone's favorite grocery store. They had the freshest fruits and vegetables in town. The staff was especially friendly. Stone was convinced that it all started with Mike Wages, the manager. He was always friendly and went out of his way to speak to all of his regular customers. Stone picked up some snacks, fresh bread, milk and lots of cereal. Cereal could sustain kids almost indefinitely.

Everyone was quiet on the short ride from Publix to home. Stone took Paula to her room and made sure that she was comfortable. Then he went back to get the groceries out of the car and put them up. To his surprise, Steven had already brought all the groceries in and put them away.

"Thanks, Steven," Stone said. He walked over and hugged his son. It felt good and Stone realized that he had not done that enough. "I really appreciate your help. It means a lot to me."

"You're welcome, Dad. I know you've got a lot on your plate right now."

"Don't you worry about that," Stone said. "Things are going to get better. Trust me."

"I do, Dad. You are the most trustworthy person I know."

That comment stopped Stone cold. Was this whole deal worth breaking everyone's trust in Stone? Was his using other people's money, without their permission, a trustworthy thing to do? Stone's head was spinning with all these thoughts, when Kathy's words put all of them to rest. "Stone, do whatever it takes to take care of our kids."

Stone smiled at Steven, ruffled his hair and then headed to his room to change.

*****

At 12:15 pm, Stone knocked on Steven's door.

"Come in," Steven answered.

"I've got to run over to the park and work for a couple of hours. Paula should sleep while I'm gone. I've got my cell phone. You can call me if you need me."

"What? I thought you were staying home today. What if Paula starts hurting again?" Steven was obviously surprised that Stone was leaving.

"Don't worry." Stone assured him. "The doctor said she should be fine until later tonight. I've got to go to work. I am out of sick days. Ms. Janet is going to stop by and check on you and your sister. I put her cell phone number on the kitchen counter."

"OK, Dad. I'll call if anything happens."

Of course, Stone was not headed to work. He was on his way to pick up Eli and turn in the winning ticket. With Paula's health worsening, Stone now knew he had no choice. He needed the money as soon as he could get it. He hated deceiving his son, but under these circumstances, Stone could justify telling a little white lie.

*****

Stone looked in on Paula on his way out. She was sleeping peacefully.

Don't worry, he thought, *Daddy's going to take care of you.*

Chapter 15

Friday

As Stone and Eli had agreed, they met at 1:00 pm at Riverside Park. The city had built this park in 2005. It was the site of great events such as the Riverside Sounds Concert Series, the B98.5 Movie Under the Stars and the Back to the Chattahoochee Canoe and Kayak Race and Festival. It boasted not one but two themed playgrounds, a water spraying playground, a concert area complete with a large grass area for picnicking and a boardwalk out to the Chattahoochee River.

From the Riverside Park dock it was possible to see where Vickery Creek (also called Big Creek) flowed into the Chattahoochee River. This was the site where the city's founder, Roswell King, had crossed the river on his way to

Dahlonega, Georgia to start a bank during the gold rush of 1828. The beauty of the river and the surrounding area impressed Roswell King so much that he vowed to return with his family and build a home and, in 1838, that is just what Roswell King did. And the rest, as they say, is history.

Riverside Park was also the trailhead for the Roswell River Walk. This 7-mile multi-use trail was heavily used by walkers, joggers and bicyclists, and Stone knew they could leave Eli's car there for several hours without it being noticed.

As Eli was walking toward the Trooper, Stone noticed Eli was limping a little, walking more slowly than usual and wearing sunglasses. At first, Stone did not think anything of it, but when Eli did not begin to chatter away, he knew something was wrong.

"Why the dark glasses and the silent treatment, Eli?" Stone asked.

Eli slowly turned to look at Stone. He pulled the glasses off to reveal two bloodshot eyes and one black eye.

"What happened?" Stone asked. He had left Eli less than 12 hours ago and Eli's eyes were fine then.

"Nothing I can't handle," growled Eli.

"Come on, Eli. If we are going to be partners, you have to tell me everything. I can't afford any surprises."

Eli looked away and put his sunglasses back on. "I went to Johnson's Bar last night for a quick beer. Some sorry ass son of a bitch kept saying how sorry the Atlanta Falcons were. He just kept on. So finally I called him out. Long story short, we went outside and discussed the subject a little more intently. Let's just say the Falcons' reputation is safe."

Stone was livid. "You went to a bar last night? I thought you had to get home because of your babysitter. No wait, your mom is your babysitter. You took my $50 and spent it on booze?

Before Eli could answer, Stone realized there was a bigger problem. "Did you tell anyone about our deal?"

"Of course not," Eli answered. "What do you think I am, stupid?"

Stone thought, *Of course I think you are stupid*, but he said, "No, I don't think you're stupid. But for the kind of money we are dealing with here, a lot of folks would sell their souls and their mamas to the devil. You're not starting our partnership on a real good note. I got to know I can trust you, Eli."

Eli did not respond. Stone decided to drop it, but he couldn't stop the gnawing feeling in the pit of his stomach.

What do you think I am, stupid?

*****

The drive from Roswell to downtown Atlanta was uneventful. The traffic was light on Georgia 400 due to the snow. Almost all the snow was gone off the highways, but most folks were apparently staying in. Due to the light traffic, only two of the toll booths were open on Georgia Highway 400. Georgia 400 was the only toll road in Atlanta. It linked downtown Atlanta and the northern suburban towns of Sandy Springs, Roswell, Alpharetta, Johns Creek and Milton. It had been labeled the "Hospitality Highway" by the local convention and visitors bureaus to entice folks to stop often and enjoy the hospitality of the locals.

Stone had completely forgotten to bring cash for the toll. He did not have any cash on him at all. He was sure Eli did not, either, especially after his night of boozing. His plan was to beg forgiveness from the toll worker and hope that they would let him through on the promise to pay later.

The lady in the car in front of him dropped her dollar bill when giving it to the toll worker. She tried to open the door and get out but there was not enough room between the car and the toll booth for the car door to open. After watching a minute or so of the lady continually trying to open the door, Stone finally put the Trooper in park and got out to get the lady's dollar. The lady did not even thank Stone when he handed her the wet dollar.

"People are just so ungrateful," Stone commented as he returned to the Trooper. "Is a simple 'Thank you' too much to ask for?"

Eli was either asleep behind his sunglasses or totally ignoring Stone.

As Stone pulled up to the toll booth, the toll worker said, "Oh sir, you don't have to pay. The lady you got the dollar for paid your toll. She was so embarrassed that she could hardly speak. You are good to go through."

Timing...the key to life.

Chapter 16

Friday

As Stone and Eli arrived at the Georgia Lottery office, the tension was mounting. Up till now, Stone could turn back. He could just turn the ticket over to the lottery group and they would soon forget about the delay in getting their money. But once they handed the ticket over to the lottery officials, there was no turning back.

It was, as they say, time to fish or cut bait.

Stone pulled into a space where he could easily see the front door of the office building. He wanted to make sure he could see Eli go into the office, and more importantly, see him come out. Stone put the Trooper into park and turned off the engine. It was now 2:10 pm.

Neither man spoke for a minute. Stone finally broke the silence. "Ok, Eli. One last time. Can I trust you?"

Eli pulled off his sunglasses and turned to look Stone dead in the eye. "Ok, Stone. One last time. Yes, you can trust me."

Eli continued without breaking the gaze. "I'm sorry about last night. I just needed to take the edge off. You've got to admit, getting a $3,000,000 gig can put you on edge. Stone, I need this money as bad as you do. I've got a bigger closet with far more skeletons in it than you do. Yes, you can trust me."

Stone sighed, "Thank you for that, Eli. I don't mean to doubt you. But this is big and my little girl's life depends on you right now."

"Quit your worrying. We're going to save your little girl," Eli said, and added with a smile, "and my ass."

Stone reached into his shirt pocket and pulled out the multi-million dollar ticket. Stone looked at it one last time, and then handed it to Eli. Eli took it and slipped it into his coat pocket.

Stone nervously asked, "Do you have your driver's license and social security card?"

According to the Georgia State Lottery website, winners were required to present two forms of identification. They preferred a valid driver's license and an original social security card. Stone had told Eli several times to be sure and bring these two items specifically.

Eli answered, "Yes, I have them both."

"Good luck," Stone said and smiled at his own dry wit. Though Eli was about to walk into the office that based its business on luck, Eli did not pick up on the joke.

As they shook hands, Eli said, "Relax Stone, I got this."

With that, Eli got out and headed towards the lottery office entrance.

*****

The lobby of the Georgia Lottery office looks like the entrance to a casino in Biloxi, Mississippi. Everywhere you looked there were enlarged photos of folks winning money. The smaller amounts of $500,000 to $2,000,000 were in the smaller frames near the entrance door. The mid-range winners, $3,000,000 to $10,000,000, were in larger frames and grouped together in the middle of the lobby. The big winners, over $10,000,000, were in gold frames over the receptionist desk. The art lights, hanging from the ceiling and shining directly on the photos, gave the images a look that made them resemble a shrine to the money god.

Eli walked up to the receptionist, who was on the phone. She glanced at him and then quickly returned her attention to whoever was on the phone. It was obviously a personal call. She was an extremely attractive lady in her late twenties. She was dressed in a smart green business suit. Eli could not help but look at her short skirt that had ridden up her thigh a little. She noticed Eli noticing and quickly made the necessary adjustments. Eli wondered if she would have made those adjustments if she had known how rich he was about to be.

"May I help you?" she asked when she finally finished her phone call.

"Yes you can, Kay." Eli had taken a real good look at the name tag she was wearing on her chest. "I'm here for my money."

"Excuse me?" Kay asked. Eli's statement obviously caught her off guard.

"I have the winning Mega Millions ticket." Eli stated confidently as he pulled the golden ticket out of his coat pocket.

"Oh my," gasped Kay. "Usually winners call ahead of time so we know they are coming. I'll call upstairs. I'm sure Ms. Delaney McFellow will want to come down and meet you."

Eli was cool and collected. "Do what you have to do, but could you hurry? I'm ready to get out of here and start spending my money." Eli liked this new position of power.

Kay picked up the phone and quietly, but excitedly, spoke into the receiver. Whoever Kay was speaking to was obviously giving her instructions to follow.

"May I get you anything while you wait?" Kay asked as she hung up the phone.

Eli fought the urge to say something crude about what he really wanted. "I could use a beer, but I'll settle for a Coke."

"Well, we don't have any alcohol, but I can sure get you a Coke. I will be right back," Kay said. Eli guessed that Kay was from North Georgia, maybe Dalton, Georgia, by the way she made the word "right" sound like it was three syllables long.

Kay returned with a 20 ounce bottle of Coke. She walked purposefully around the receptionist desk and sashayed toward Eli who had taken a seat and was flipping through the latest copy of Atlanta Magazine. Eli knew his picture would be on the cover of the next edition.

Kay handed him the bottle of Coke. Eli could not tell if she kept her hand on the bottle longer than she should have on purpose or on accident.

Before he could stop himself, Eli asked, "Are you married, Kay?"

"Why no, I'm not," Kay answered shyly.

Eli was now on a roll. "It sounds like you're from up around Dalton and I would have thought one of those rich carpet guys would have hand-picked you by now." Dalton, Georgia is the carpet capital of the world. More carpet is produced in Dalton than anywhere else in the world. There are more millionaires per capita in Dalton than anywhere else in the United States. There are also more divorces in Dalton per capita than anywhere else in the United States.

"Actually," Kay began, no doubt flirting now, "I'm from Rocky Face." Rocky Face is a small town in North Georgia, about 15 miles from Dalton. "I'm waiting on Mr. Right. I know he's out there and one day he is just going to walk right into my life."

Eli was enjoying the flirting. Kay was nervously playing with her long blond hair and shifting her weight from one foot to the other. But before he could respond, the door behind the desk opened. Out came an entourage of executives. There were a total of six people; it was clear that the one female in the group was in charge.

She walked right up to Eli and introduced herself. "I'm Delaney McFellow, President and CEO of the Georgia Lottery Corporation. I understand that you are our big winner."

"Nice to meet you Delaney, I mean Ms. McFellow," Eli responded.

"Oh, please, call me Delaney. We need to take you back and verify the ticket so we can get you your money. Of course, we'll have to take your picture with the big check. Will that be ok?"

"Great, Delaney. That's what I came for," Eli said, regaining some of his confidence from a moment ago.

As he followed the group back out of the lobby, Eli glanced back at Kay. She winked and smiled.

Eli thought, *I could get used to this type of treatment.*

*****

Three hours later, Eli was escorted back to the lobby area. Before he left, Kay slipped him a note with her phone number on it.

Yep, Eli thought as he headed out to the parking lot, *I could get used to this type of treatment.*

*****

Stone felt his heart jump when he saw Eli carrying the big oversized check.

"We're rich!" Eli yelled as he literally jumped into the Trooper.

"When do we get the real money?" Stone asked.

"It will be in ours in two business days," Eli answered. "Come next week, my friend, we will be rich. They are going to direct deposit the money into my bank account on Tuesday. Are you ready for this? The final total was $147,000,000.00. WE – ARE – RICH!"

"I can't believe it. This whole thing is going to work," Stone said out loud, but he was really talking to himself.

Eli couldn't keep from smiling. "We need to celebrate. Let's go have a drink!"

Stone's mood changed immediately. "We can't. I have to go home and take care of my sick child."

"OK," Eli dejectedly agreed. "I guess we should wait until we really have the money."

"That's a good plan," Stone said. "There will be plenty of time for celebrating and partying. Right now I just want to get home to Paula and check in with Dr. Ishmael."

It was now 5:00 pm on Friday afternoon. Usually on Friday at that time, Georgia Highway 400 would be a parking lot. But with the snow that had fallen, the traffic was abnormally light.

Stone knew they were lucky today. The snow had greatly reduced the traffic. The snow had closed the schools, which allowed him to be home when Paula's cramps had started. The snow had kept the media off the lottery story. The snow had come at just the right time.

Timing...the key to life.

*****

As Stone dropped off Eli at his car, he reminded Eli to lay low for a while. "It's important that we stay out of the lime light as long and as much as we can. The fewer questions we have to answer, the better off we are."

"No problem," Eli said. "I can be invisible when I want to be."

Chapter 17

Friday/Saturday

Eli was on top of the world. He had tried to sit home and lay low like he had promised Stone, but he just could not.

He needed to take the edge off. Eli had decided to celebrate quietly. His plan was to have no more than two beers, calm down, relax and then go home. He would not talk to anyone.

He had wanted to go earlier in the evening, but as luck would have it, his mom was late getting home from her Sunday school party. When she finally got home around 10:00 pm, he almost did not go out. However, after he told his mom about winning the lottery and that he was going to get

$3,000,000.00 out of the deal, she had almost driven him crazy with questions and he decided to get out of the house.

*****

The news was out that someone from Roswell had won the lottery. Eli smiled as he watched the 11:00 pm news on the TV above the bar. He was sitting in the upstairs bar at Andretti's Karting and Games. This indoor entertainment center featured three different inside go-cart tracks, a large game room, a climbing wall, a high ropes course, a restaurant, a comedy club, a meeting space and a bar that overlooked the entire facility.

The TV was tuned to Channel 46, which was the local CBS network station. The lead story was the local winner of one of the largest jackpots in Mega Millions history.

Of course, there was no footage of the winner, but Eli's name was now showing on the screen as the local reporter was broadcasting live from the Corner Grocery.

Eli finished his third Miller High Life. He had promised himself that he would only have two, but had stayed for a third because he thought that the good looking blonde in the corner had been trying to make eye contact with him. But just after he ordered his third beer, a rather large guy had come in and sat down with her.

He glanced up at the clock; it was a couple of minutes after midnight. Saturday did not look like it was going to be as lucky as Friday was.

He left a good tip for the bartender; after all, he was rich, now. As he was leaving, he decided he needed to use the facilities. He could have made it home, but decided, *why wait?* Now he could do what he wanted when he wanted; why not start now?

*****

After taking care of business, as Eli was coming down the hallway that opened up to the lobby and the exit doors, he literally ran into Carter King.

Timing…the key to life.

Eli and Carter knew each other, but just in passing. They had common friends, but had never spent any time together. Eli did know that Carter was a member of Stone's lottery group.

"Well, if it's not Roswell's newest millionaire. You're quite the celebrity around here. I guess congratulations are in order," Carter remarked with a wink.

Eli had not expected to run into anyone he knew, and to run into someone from Stone's lottery group was just bad luck. Eli knew his best bet was to get out quick.

"Thanks." Eli said. "I'm trying to keep a low profile. You don't know who you can trust these days."

Carter winked at Eli again and said, "You're telling me. I feel like I've been cheated out of a lot lately. You better be careful. You know there are a lot of folks who would lie, cheat, steal, kidnap and kill for that kind of money.

"I was just having a couple of beers in private before the craziness starts. I was hoping that no one would recognize me." Eli was struggling with what to say.

"Don't worry, Eli. Your secret is safe with me." Carter winked again.

"Thanks Carter. I've had a long day. I'm gonna get out of here." Eli knew he needed to cut off the conversation.

Carter, however, was not in a hurry. "Maybe you can help me out. I didn't get a chance to check all my tickets for the Mega Millions. Since you won I assume you know the winning numbers. What were they?"

Eli was in trouble. He did not have a clue what the winning numbers were. He had looked at the ticket, but he had no recollection whatsoever as to what the winning numbers were. All he could think to say was, "I don't remember. They were just quick pick numbers. I didn't pick them so I don't remember them."

"That's strange you don't remember the numbers." Carter was leaning forward a little now. "Seems to me a man should remember the six numbers that made him a millionaire. I know I would."

Eli tried to recover. "If you knew me better, you would know that I am not good at numbers or remembering."

"Yeah, sure," Carter replied, obviously not buying the explanation. "By the way, where did you buy the winning ticket at? I bet that store loves you."

Eli was getting deeper and deeper. Stone had not mentioned where he had bought the ticket. Eli decided to play it safe. "I bought tickets at Publix, the Corner Grocery and the Shell Station across from City Hall." Eli had seen Stone in all three of those places.

"Good to see you, Eli," Carter reached out his hand. "Just remember if you decide that all that money is too much for you, I know a few guys at the park who would love to have their fair share of it."

"I'll keep that in mind," Eli said as he shook Carter's hand.

Carter watched Eli until he was out the door and out of sight.

Chapter 18

Saturday

Eli's mother, Kaylee, woke up Eli by banging on his bedroom door. Eli had not slept well. Between enjoying the idea of being a millionaire and worrying about his conversation with Carter, he had tossed and turned all night. He felt like he had just closed his eyes.

"What do you want, Mama?" Eli said. "It's Saturday. I don't have to get up today."

"Yeah, you do," answered Kaylee. "There are news trucks outside and they have already been knocking on the front door. Mr. Tate next door has already called the police because the Channel 5 van was blocking his driveway. You know how he hates FOX news."

"OK, Mama. I'll get dressed and take care of them." Eli quickly picked up his phone and called Stone.

Stone answered on the first ring. "Hello."

"Stone, it's Eli. The TV stations are all over the place. They are parked on the grass. What should I do?"

"Stay calm, Eli." Stone knew this was coming, so he was ready. "Best thing you can do is go out and let them interview you. Just keep your answers short. Don't try to be funny or witty. You want to be boring so they will get bored and wrap things up quick."

"OK, I understand," Eli said. "Hey, by the way, where did you buy the winning ticket and what were the numbers?"

Stone hesitated for a second. "I bought the ticket at the Corner Grocery and the numbers were 2, 12, 15, 27, 29 and the Mega Ball number was 2. What made you ask those questions?"

Now it was Eli's turn to be ready for a question. "I was thinking last night what questions the reporters might ask me and those are the ones I came up with." Eli had decided to not tell Stone about his run-in with Carter. No reason to upset Stone. He had enough to worry about as it was.

Stone was impressed. Maybe Eli was capable of pulling this off. "Remember Eli, use the KISS method."

"The what method?" Eli asked.

"KISS. Keep It Simple, Stupid."

Eli took offense to the comment. "Don't call me stupid."

Stone laughed, "I didn't call you stupid. That's just a saying. Just a reminder that the simple answers are always the best."

Eli was not convinced, but he let it go.

"I'll call you when I'm done, *partner*," Eli said.

Stone didn't like the way he said partner, but Eli hung up before he could respond.

Chapter 19

Saturday

Stone watched the midday news. He flipped between all the local stations. When all was said and done, he was pleased.

Eli had done a great job. He answered all the reporters' questions in brief, concise statements. When it was over, Eli came across as a guy who had just won $147,000,000.00. He was all smiles and when asked what was the first thing he was going to do with his new found fortune, he answered, "Brenda and me are going to Disney World!"

After the news, Stone called Dr. Ishmael. Everything was set for Stone and Paula to leave for Mexico on Friday. The doctor had made all the arrangements. He had booked the flights, secured the doctors for the procedure, arranged for the donor kidney and made arrangements for a place for Stone to stay across the street from the hospital. Stone could pay Dr. Ishmael in full when the lottery money came in on Tuesday.

Now Stone's biggest problem was Steven. He had been so focused on Paula, he had forgotten about making any arrangements for Steven to stay in Roswell with someone. Stone had no immediate family in the area. His dad had died of a heart attack when Stone was 9. His mom, Sandy, had remarried and now lived in Seattle, Washington. He only saw her twice a year. She always flew back to Georgia at Christmas each year, and Stone and the kids flew out to Washington State during the summer. But his mom worked full time as a school teacher and could not take off the time to stay with Steven. He could send his son to Seattle, but that would be extremely difficult on Steven to change schools in the middle of the year and so far away from home.

Stone's only hope was Janet.

The difficult part would be to explain to Janet how he suddenly got the money to pay for the trip and the operation. He did not want to tell her the truth because Stone really, really liked Janet. He was afraid if he told her about keeping all the money that belonged to the lottery group that she would think that he was dishonest and would not have anything else to do with him.

And Stone really, really liked Janet.

Stone came up with a story. It would go like this: Years ago Stone had done Eli a huge favor. He had kept him out of jail. So far, so true. Now Eli had won the lottery and wanted to repay Stone. Stone had saved his life. Now Eli was going to save Paula. Not exactly true, but not entirely a lie. Stone decided to go with the story.

He called Janet at home. The answering machine picked up. Stone left a message asking her if she could call him when she got in.

*****

A half hour later, Stone's phone rang. It was Janet. Stone wasted no time telling Janet the arrangements Dr. Ishmael had made for Paula. He explained how Eli had offered to pay for Paula's surgery because of an old favor Stone had done for Eli.

"We've been praying for a miracle and it has happened," explained Stone.

"That is such wonderful, exciting news! It could not have happened to a more deserving family," Janet said.

"But," Stone said slowly, "I've still got a problem."

"No you don't," said Janet. "Steven can stay with me."

"How in the world did you know that I was going to ask you that?" A surprised Stone asked.

"Because you are easy to read, Stone. You were so wrapped up in saving Paula, you forgot that you were going to have to leave Steven. I love that you were so focused on saving your daughter that everything else had to take a back seat. That is what true love is all about." Janet said all of this so matter-of-factly that it brought a tear to Stone's eye.

"I don't know what to say." Stone was almost speechless.

"You don't have to say anything. Maybe we can all go out tonight and we will talk about this as families," Janet suggested easily.

"That's a great idea. Let's meet at Alessio's at 7:00 pm and we'll work out the details."

"Great," Janet cooed. "It's a date."

Stone really, really like Janet.

*****

Around 4:00 pm, Paula had another round of cramps. They lasted almost thirty minutes. When the cramps finally abated, Paula was completely worn out.

As Paula was falling back to sleep, Stone mentioned that he had talked to Janet and they were planning to meet her and her kids at Alessio's, but that maybe they should cancel.

Paula became wide awake. "Don't you dare, Dad! You know I love the Stromboli. Besides, I really want to see Jade.

"OK, baby. Why don't you take your medicines and lay down? I'll wake you when it's time to go.

"OK, Dad. I love you."

"I love you, too, Paula."

Chapter 20

Saturday

Eli's mother began banging on his bedroom door again. "Eli, are you in there?"

"Yea, Mama, where else would I be?" Eli was resting and almost asleep.

"Well, you got company. Some guy named Barrett is here to see you."

Oh crap, Eli thought. He had forgotten to call Barrett. At least now he would be able to pay him off and get him out of his life.

Eli made his way into the living room. He found Kaylee and Barrett sitting on the couch, talking as if they were old friends. Barrett was showing Kaylee pictures of his kids.

"Hey Mom, me and Barrett have some business to discuss. Could we have a little privacy?"

Kaylee took offense to being asked to leave. "Privacy, spivacy. What kind of business are you doing that you can't talk about it in front of your mom?"

Eli did not want to make his mama mad. "Mama, it's nothing important or bad. You would just be bored."

"OK, I know when I'm not wanted. I bet Barrett here don't treat his mom like this, do you?"

Barrett played along with Kaylee. "No ma'am, I would never ask my mama to leave her own living room."

"You're sweet, Barrett. You ought to talk to Eli about respect." As Kaylee left the room, she was mumbling to herself.

When they were alone, Barrett smiled and said, "Hey, rich boy. I saw you on TV."

"Yeah, I guess everyone saw me. I'll have your $750,000.00 on Tuesday. Then we'll be square," Eli said.

Barrett's voice became cold. "Well, that's the thing I wanted to talk to you about. With your new found fortune, our interest rate went up. Your fee is now $5,000,000.00."

"What? You can't do that," Eli said harshly.

Barrett took a minute to answer. When he did, there was sharpness in his voice. "Listen carefully, Eli. I've carried you for a long time. I've been easy on you. You know I could have broken an arm or leg for what you've owed me. I've killed people for less money than you've owed me. So the way I look at it, you owe me a little respect and a great deal of interest. Besides man, you've got $147,000,000.00. What's a measly $5,000,000.00 to you? That's pocket change for you."

Eli was stuck. Of course, he could not tell Barrett that he was only getting $3,000,000 out of the deal. And there was no way that Barrett was going to get all of his money. But Barrett was not someone to play with. Eli knew of a couple of guys that turned up missing after disappointing Barrett.

"Look Barrett, I owe you $750,000.00 and that's what I'm going to pay you. I will throw in an extra $250,000.00 and make it a cool $1,000,000.00, but that's all. A deal is a deal. Ain't that what you always say?" Eli was getting pissed.

Barrett was getting pissed, too. "Yeah, that's what I always say. But I think I deserve more money than that. I've carried you a long time. You know, I got people I answer to, too and they are asking questions. And believe me, Eli, you don't want to know the answers to the questions they are asking."

Eli did not like being pushed and his new found fortune was giving him a little confidence. "Well, Barrett, I guess the questions and answers are your problem, not mine."

"Make no mistake, Eli, it's your problem."

Eli ignored the comment. "I'll have your money on Tuesday. That's well ahead of your deadline. I'll call you when I get the money and we'll decide where to meet." Eli was done now. He stood up and walked to the front door and opened it.

As Barrett was moving through the door, he said, "Be careful, Eli; lots of folks are watching you. You're a celebrity now and all kinds of things happen to celebrities and their family and friends."

With that, Barrett smiled, shook his head and walked slowly to his car.

As Eli was watching Barrett drive away, Eli's daughter, Brenda, came up behind him and asked, "Who was that big man, Daddy?"

"Just a guy I work with sometimes. Nobody, really," Eli answered.

"Well, whoever he was, Grandma sure does like him. She said he was nice and respectful. But she sure is mad at you. She's in the kitchen just a-fussing."

Eli lowered and slowly shook his head and smiled. "I'll go make up with her. I'll remind her that we are rich. Maybe that will make her happy."

"Whatever, Daddy. I'm going on the porch to have a tea party."

Chapter 21

Saturday

Alessio's was a favorite of the folks that live on the west side of Roswell. It had great Italian food and was voted "Best NY Pizza" by <u>Atlanta Magazine.</u> As was usual for a Saturday night, there was a wait for a party of 6.

Stone, Steven and Paula arrived a few minutes early and got their name on the wait list. Janet and her kids were running late. When they arrived at 7:20 pm, the waitress was just showing Stone to their booth. They got lucky and got one of the two big booths in the back, close to the small game room that the kids liked to play in as they waited for their food. An oversized picture of John Wayne dressed as a cowboy kept a close eye on what was happening.

The waitress, a cute, young girl named Tara, approached to take their drink order. But because they were regulars, they already knew what they wanted to eat as well. They ordered 4 Strombolis for the entire group. Stone and Janet each ordered a small salad. Everybody drank sweet tea. As soon as the waitress left to place their order, the kids were ready to head to the game room.

"Wait. Slow down," Stone said. "We've got something we need to talk to all you kids about." Stone looked nervously at Janet. She gave him a reassuring smile.

"What gives, Dad?" Steven asked. He always wanted to cut to the chase.

Stone took a deep breath before he spoke. "Good news, guys. We have made arrangements to get Paula the operation she needs to get well."

"That's great!" Steven said. "Now can I have a couple of dollars for the game room?"

Stone smiled at Steven. He did not focus on any one thing for too long. Stone continued, "Hold on, there's more. The operation will take place in Mexico. We have to leave next week."

Before Stone could go further, Janet jumped in. "Paula getting well is great news. And guess what guys? Steven gets to come stay with us while Stone and Paula are in Mexico."

It took a minute for what Janet had said to sink in.

The first to speak was Colby. "That's great. I've always wanted a big brother." With that, Colby turned towards his little sister, Jade, and stuck out his tongue.

A smile came across Steven's face. "Great! I'm sure we'll have fun." Steven had a crush on Janet and everyone but Steven knew it.

Jade was also smiling since she had a crush on Steven.

It seemed everyone was happy except Paula. Stone turned to her and asked, "What's wrong, baby girl?"

With that, tears started swelling up in Paula's eyes. Stone quickly gave Steven $10 and told him to take Jade and Colby and go play video games. All three went eagerly.

Stone looked at his baby girl and asked quietly, "What's the matter, Paula?"

"I'm scared Daddy. What if I die in Mexico?" Paula asked. She looked so small.

"Don't worry, Paula," Stone said. "Dr. Ishmael said the doctors that will be making you better are the best. You trust Dr. Ishmael, don't you?"

"Yeah, but I don't want to die like Mommy." Paula was still crying.

This broke Stone's heart. He reached over and hugged Paula and said, "You don't need to worry. I'll take care of you. We're going to stay together forever."

"Promise?" Her crying was slowing.

"Of course. You and me, forever and ever, amen." Stone sang the last part in his best Randy Travis voice. Randy

Travis is a well known country singer who was one of Stone's favorites.

"Thanks Daddy. You're the best. Could I go play now?" Stone was always amazed at how quickly kids could go from crying to laughing. It only took a kind word from the right person at the right time.

Timing...the key to life.

When Paula had left, Stone looked at Janet and said simply, "Thanks."

"You would do the same for me," was her reply. And Stone knew she was right.

"I don't think I'll ever be able to repay you." Stone said honestly.

"Don't worry, I'll think of something. Too bad we don't have a babysitter tonight," Janet said with a slight gleam in her eye.

That comment caught Stone completely off guard. What did she mean by that? Stone had strong feelings about Janet and he wondered if she felt the same way. He had honestly not thought about having a relationship with anyone for a long time. But Janet brought out the old feelings of the need to have a soul mate.

Could she possibly be having the same thoughts? Janet's husband had been killed while on a business trip four years earlier. The small private plane he was flying in had crashed on its approach to the Myrtle Beach, South Carolina airport. All three people aboard had died.

"Yes, too bad we don't have a babysitter tonight," Stone repeated. "Maybe when we get back from Mexico, you and I can spend some quality time together."

Janet's eyes never left Stone's. "I'd like that. I'd like that a lot."

Stone really, really liked Janet.

Chapter 22

Sunday

Stone decided to sleep in on Sunday. He knew the kids needed the rest, and so did he. He finally got up around 8:30 am and as usual, got the coffee going and then went to get the newspaper.

He waited until he got back to the kitchen before he took the newspaper out of the plastic sleeve. He was hoping that the Lottery winner would be forgotten, but as he opened the front page, his hopes were dashed.

There was Eli, front and center. The headlines read:

The $147,000,000 Man

The story that accompanied the picture was short. It talked about Eli's age, occupation (or lack thereof would be more appropriate) and how he only bought one ticket. He was quoted saying that he usually did not play the Mega-Million's game, but just decided to buy a ticket at the Corner Grocery on his way home.

"Timing is the key to life," Eli was quoted in the article.

All in all, Stone thought the newspaper article was good. He was confident that the news coverage was pretty much over. Now all he had to do was wait for the money to be deposited into Eli's account, then get the cash, and his problems would be solved.

Stone decided to wait and call Eli later in the afternoon. He would make arrangements for them to meet at the Bank of North Georgia on Monday to work out the details. Both Eli and Stone were customers of the Bank of North Georgia, so the exchange should be relatively easy.

Stone felt himself relaxing. Everything was falling into place. They had the money they needed. The arrangements had been made in Mexico. Steven was staying with Janet. And Janet had said she liked the idea of them spending more time together.

Stone could not believe his luck. Things were working out great. Everything was falling into place in just the right order. He was simply in the right places at the right times.

Chapter 23

Sunday

Brenda was playing on the front porch. She liked to pretend that she was hosting a world famous tea party. Brenda had quite an imagination. She loved to have special guests over for High Tea. On any given day, she might have the Queen of England, Hanna Montana and Johnny Depp all sitting with her enjoying a nice High Tea.

Last Christmas, Kaylee, Brenda's grandmother, had taken Brenda to the fancy High Tea hosted at Historic Bulloch Hall in Roswell. This annual holiday event featured fancy finger food served by waitresses and waiters in period costumes. The tea was served in real china from sterling silver tea pots. Brenda had fallen in love with the idea of High Tea. She was becoming quite the hostess.

Even though it was cold, Brenda enjoyed the outdoor tea parties to the indoor ones. Everybody on the street was used to seeing Brenda on the porch with her "tea friends".

She had a tea party every day.

Chapter 24

Sunday

Around 4:30 pm, Paula began having cramps again. After 30 minutes, with no let up in the pain, Stone called Dr. Ishmael's cell phone number. The doctor picked up on the second ring.

Stone quickly updated the doctor on the cramps from yesterday and what was currently happening.

"Stone, there is nothing more we can do now. We just have to let the cramps pass. Do you still have the medicine I prescribed?" The doctor was trying to remain calm.

"Yes, Doc. I think we still have 8 or 9 pills left." Stone said with exhaustion in his voice.

"OK. I'll call you in another prescription. I want you to double up on the pills. That should help keep the cramps to a minimum. In the meantime, keep her laying down as much as possible."

"OK Doc. Is everything set for Friday?" Stone asked.

"Yes, I've talked with the hospital and the doctor. I also have spoken to the owner of the condo near the hospital. It is all set. You should receive your confirmation for the flight tomorrow."

"Ok, Doc. I can't thank you enough. You are literally a life saver." Stone was almost getting chocked up.

"No problem," The doctor answered. "I got to go."

Stone returned to Paula's room. The cramps were beginning to fade. He gave her two pills and told her to stay in bed and rest.

Stone sat on the side of the bed and rubbed Paula's head until she fell asleep. Friday needed to hurry up and get here. He was ready for his baby girl to be well.

Chapter 25

Monday

Stone called Bart Henderson at 7:00 am on Monday morning. He told Bart that Paula was still sick and he would not be in for a few days. He said he understood that he would have to take the days without pay. He promised to call and give daily updates on Paula.

*****

As planned, Stone met Eli at the Bank of North Georgia at 10:00 am. The Bank of North Georgia was the largest local bank in Roswell. Unlike most local banks in Georgia, It had survived the economic crisis. The bank actually knew their customers and did not make loans to folks that could not afford them.

The bank, which sat at the corner of Highway 9 and Highway 92, was located on the site of the old Lebanon Baptist Church. Lebanon was the first church in Roswell to allow slaves to sit in the balcony on Sundays.

They met with Trevor Collins to discuss the details of the money switch. Mr. Collins was excited about the $147,000,000.00 deposit. However, his mood changed when Eli told him that they would be immediately moving $142,000,000.00 out of his account. He breathed a sigh of relief when Stone told him the $142,000,000.00 would be put into another Bank of North Georgia under Stone's name.

"Now," Stone added, "the most important part. You cannot tell anyone about the transfer. Can you do that?"

"Of course," Mr. Collins said, "discretion is one of our specialties."

"Thank you, Mr. Collins." Stone continued, "But I must press upon the need for complete secrecy. If you cannot guarantee us of that, we must go somewhere else. I mean no disrespect or offense by stating this important aspect twice."

"No offense taken and no need to apologize for making sure you are properly protected." Mr. Collins' expression never changed. "With the amount of money we are dealing with here, you must be extremely careful. I give you my personal guarantee that your accounts, their balances and your transactions are your business and no one else's. I will personally handle all of your transactions in the privacy of my office."

Mr. Collins stated that the lottery money should be available from the Lottery Corporation by 2:00 pm on Tuesday. Stone and Eli made a follow-up appointment at 2:30 pm on Tuesday to get the money in the right places.

*****

As they were leaving the Bank of North Georgia, Stone and Eli were both pretty happy. In their excitement, neither noticed the audience they had attracted.

At one end of the parking lot sat Barrett and another, bigger man in Barrett's Mercedes 350E. They were carefully watching Stone and Eli.

Meanwhile, at the opposite end of the parking lot, Carter was watching from his Chevy Avalanche. Nobody noticed him.

Chapter 26

Monday

Brenda was hosting her daily tea party. Today's invitation list included the Queen of England, Taylor Swift, and Dora the Explorer. All the guests had arrived and were seated, when a Mercedes 350E drove past the house. Of course, Brenda paid no attention as the car slowly made its way down the street and turned around. It drove slowly back past the house again.

Inside the house, the phone rang. Kaylee, Eli's mom, answered it. A volunteer from Kaylee's church was conducting a telephone survey regarding Sunday school times and schedules. Kaylee did not recognize the person calling and she was not aware that the church was thinking about making changes to the schedule. She liked the way things were and took her time explaining to the nice young man why things needed to stay the way they were. The caller had promised that the survey would not last more than 5 or 6 minutes, but Kaylee kept him on the phone for a good 12 minutes.

After she was convinced that she had explained her thoughts on any unneeded changes at the church, she walked out to the front porch to tell Brenda to wash up for dinner.

Kaylee was surprised that Brenda was not on the porch with the rest of her tea party guests.

Kaylee asked The Queen of England, "Have you seen Brenda? She is supposed to be out here with y'all."

Of course, The Queen of England did not answer. Kaylee stepped down the porch steps and walked out to the street. She looked both up and down the street, but did not see Brenda. Next, she walked around the house and looked in the back yard.

Again, no Brenda.

Kaylee picked up her pace as she ran back to the front of the house. As she was running, she began yelling, "Brenda! Brenda! Where are you, girl?"

But there was no answer to her question.

Kaylee went from house to house on the street asking if anyone had seen Brenda. No one had seen her.

Now, almost in a panic, Kaylee ran back to her house. She was out of breath when she called Eli on his cell phone.

"Eli, you got to hurry home. I can't find Brenda. She was having a tea party on the porch and now she is gone. I can't find her. You need to come home."

"Mama, calm down." Eli was worried about his daughter, but he was also worried about his mother having a heart attack. "I'm on my way home. I'll be there in about 5 minutes. Just stay put till I get there."

*****

As soon as he hung up, his phone rang again. The screen read "Unknown Caller".

"Hello," Eli answered.

"Hey Eli, its Barrett."

"Barrett, I can't really talk right now. I'm in the middle of something really important." Eli was not in any mood to listen to Barrett try to talk him out of his money.

Barrett's voice became ice cold. "You need to listen to me and you need to listen carefully. I know what you are in the middle of."

Eli was confused. "What do you mean?"

"I mean, I know what you are worried about. I know where your little girl is."

Eli froze. He was no longer paying attention to the car in front of him. He had to slam on his brakes to keep from hitting the car that had stopped at the red light in front of Krispy Kreme donuts.

"Where is Brenda, you son of a bitch? If you hurt her, I'll kill you!" Eli was screaming into his cell phone.

Barrett remained calm. "You don't want to yell at me anymore. I'm the one in charge here and don't you forget it."

Eli took a couple of deep breaths as he tried to calm down. He turned his head from side to side, trying to clear it.

For some strange reason, he noticed that the "hot donuts" sign was on at Krispy Kreme, meaning that the shop had fresh, hot glazed donuts. They were Brenda's favorite.

"OK, Barrett, what do you want?"

"You know what I want. I want money. I want to renegotiate the terms of my loan to you." Barrett was enjoying being in this position of power.

Eli, on the other hand, was speechless. He had forgotten where he was. The car behind him was now blowing his horn since the light had been green for several seconds. He turned right and pulled into the Roswell Presbyterian Church parking lot.

"How much is your little girl worth, Eli?" Barrett's voice had gotten even colder, if that was possible. "If you want to see your baby girl alive, there are three things you need to do: First, do not call the cops. Any cops of any kind and Brenda dies. Second, you get all the money, all $147,000,000.00 in cash and ready by Wednesday. Third, you do what I tell you to do when I call you Wednesday. Any questions?"

Eli's head was spinning. All he wanted was Brenda. "Let me talk to Brenda," Eli demanded.

"Hold on," Barrett said.

After a few seconds, a scared voice came over the phone line. "Daddy, don't let them hurt me," Brenda was crying.

Now, Barrett was back on the phone. "Ok, Eli, you remember the three things I told you?"

"Yes."

"OK, good. I think we are making progress towards completing our deal successfully." Barrett was talking like they were negotiating the selling of a car. "You only have one shot at this, Eli. Don't blow it."

Eli was shaking. He was scared. "All the money? Did you say all the money? I thought you said $5,000,000 the other day."

Barrett was enjoying this part of the negotiations. "You should have taken that deal. Now the deal is this. All the money or Brenda dies. It's really pretty simple. So what is it, Eli? Do you want to rich or be a daddy?"

"OK. OK. I'll get the money. Just don't hurt Brenda." Eli was still shaking.

"Good choice. Talk to you Wednesday." Barrett hung up the phone.

Eli was left sitting in the parking lot. They had his little girl. What was he going to do? How was he going to tell

Stone? Whose daughter was more important? Who were they going to save?

Chapter 27

Monday

"Hello, Stone? It's me, Eli."

"What's up, Eli?" Stone was at home relaxing and playing Wii. He liked the resort game the best. He was getting pretty good at the archery game. Steven could still beat him. He always had trouble with the one where the target was on the far away island.

"We need to talk," Eli said quickly.

"What's wrong?" Stone knew from Eli's tone that something was not right.

"We need to meet. I don't want to talk about it on the phone. Meet me as soon as you can at the Taco Mac."

The Taco Mac was a sports bar chain restaurant. The Taco Mac Eli was referring to was in front of Roswell High School in the Kings Market shopping center.

"OK, Eli. I'll meet you at Taco Mac. Should I be worried?" Stone asked jokingly.

"Yeah!" Eli said louder than he wanted to. "Things have changed. I'll see you in 10 minutes."

*****

Eli was already sitting at the bar when Stone arrived at Taco Mac. He had chosen to sit at the far end of the bar which was more or less under the extra large TV screen. It also provided Eli an unobstructed view of the front door.

As Stone walked up, the bartender approached. Stone ordered a Miller High Life to match Eli's.

"OK, Eli, what's the matter?" Stone cut straight to the chase.

Eli unloaded on Stone. He told him about the gambling, Barrett, and the money he owed him. He told Stone about his visit from Barrett after the lottery winning was announced and the deal Barrett had offered that Eli had, of course, turned down. Then he dropped the bomb about the kidnapping and the demand for all the money. When he was finished he was near tears. "They've got my little girl, Stone. And they are going to kill her."

Stone was speechless. He did not know what to say or do. He just stared at Eli.

Eli repeated, "They've got my little girl. Did you hear me, Stone? They've got my little girl." The last part came out much louder than Eli had intended. The couple at the high top table next to the bar looked over. Neither Eli nor Stone paid any attention to them.

"Why didn't you tell me you were hooked up with Barrett?" Stone finally asked.

"I didn't think it mattered. It never occurred to me that they would come after the money. It never occurred to me that they would kidnap Brenda." Eli was barely hanging on. He was close to breaking down.

Stone's mind was racing. "Do you think you could get them to take less money?"

"I honestly don't know," Eli said. "My gut tells me no. Barrett don't joke around."

Stone looked past Eli for a moment. "Let me think for a minute."

As hard as Stone was thinking, nothing was coming to mind. He had heard stories about Barrett and the folks that he worked with. None of the stories were good. Stone had never dealt with folks like Barrett before. He didn't know what to do.

After 10 minutes of just looking at Eli, Stone finally said, "Let's just go home and sleep on it. We'll get back together in the morning. We'll figure something out. We'll find a way to save Brenda and Paula."

"I'm sorry Stone. I was going to live up to my end of the bargain." Eli was shaking.

"I know, Eli. We'll think of something. I'm not letting a bunch of crooks take our daughters away from us. They have no idea who they are dealing with," Stone said without expression.

Eli had never seen Stone's eyes frozen over. Eli was glad Stone was on his side.

As they left, they decided to meet on Tuesday at 12 noon at the Southern Skillet.

Chapter 28

Tuesday

Paula's scream woke Stone up at 5:35 am. Stone had not slept well, anyway. He ran to Paula's room and found her on the floor, in a fetal position, crying. He knew there was nothing he could do. He sat on the floor and simply tried to hold her the best he could.

The cramps lasted a good 45 minutes this time. As the doctor had said, the cramps were becoming more frequent and were much more intense. The medicine had helped a lot, but could not completely stop the cramps or the pain.

When Paula finally was able to relax, Stone got her another round of medicine.

Once Paula got back to sleep, Stone went into auto-pilot. He put on a whole pot of coffee. Then he walked up the driveway and got the morning paper.

When he got back into the house, he fixed his first cup of coffee and sat down at the kitchen table. But he did not start reading the paper as usual. He simply stared out the window, into the back yard.

How could things have gone so wrong so quickly?

He thought that when the Lottery group won the money that all his troubles were over. The timing was just perfect. He would get Paula well and then give the group their money, albeit a little less and a little late. It was such a simple plan. But things are never simple. Now things were spinning out of control. Not only was there a chance that Paula would not be saved, but also Eli's daughter, Brenda, was now kidnapped with no way of him knowing if she was going to survive.

Then there was the possibility that the Lottery group would not get their money. That scenario made Stone a thief, just as bad as Barrett, since the essence of a thief is a person who took other people's money without their permission.

Stone shook his head. He had to snap out of this self pity. The situation was not going to go away. If he and Eli were going to get out of this with their daughters and money intact, they had to do something.

Surely there was someone they could get to help them get out of this situation. Of course there was someone who could help, but at what cost? Stone thought of the old saying, *"The cure is worse than the disease"*.

How could the situation get any worse? Stone thought. He just had to stay focused, be positive and willing to do whatever it took to save his daughter.

*****

Janet arrived at 7:00 am. She was going to watch Paula for the day. Stone had told her he needed to go to work. He explained that he was out of PTO and sick leave. He told her he could not afford to take many more days off without pay. Janet had agreed to help out for a couple of days. She had called her friend Ginger to fill in at the school clinic for her.

Stone took Steven to school. There was always a great deal of traffic around Crabapple Middle School. It appeared that kids didn't ride the school bus anymore. Moms in SUVs and mini-vans backed up traffic on Crabapple Road as they waited to deposit their children safely at the front door.

As Steven was getting out of the Trooper, he looked back at Stone and said, "Hey Dad. Don't worry about me staying at Ms. Janet's. It'll be fun. I like her a lot. Don't do anything to make her go away. Love ya, Dad."

"I love you, Son," was all Stone could get out before Steven slammed the door and headed inside. What Steven had said hit Stone pretty hard. Janet was a great lady. She had offered to take his kid under her wing for up to six months. Not many people would do that.

"Don't do anything to make her go away." Steven's words were hanging heavy in the Trooper. All of a sudden, Stone knew what he had to do. He headed home.

Stone really, really liked Janet.

*****

When Stone walked in, Janet was cleaning the kitchen. It's hard to say who was more surprised. Stone had not expected her to do housework, although he was behind in it. And Janet did not expect Stone until late in the afternoon.

"Janet, we gotta talk," Stone said as he grabbed her hand and headed to the kitchen table. Stone came clean with the whole story. He started with his wife's final words. Then he talked about learning of Paula's rare condition.

Janet broke in and said, "Stone, I know all about this. You don't have to explain anything to me."

"Yes I do!" Stone's reply came out stronger than he would have liked. "I'm sorry, I didn't mean to say that so forcefully. There's more to the story."

He then talked about the Lottery group and the winning of the big money. Janet's eyes got big, but she did not interrupt.

He kept going with the story. He told Janet about how he saw an opportunity to save Paula, but he needed more money than his share. He explained how he had enlisted Eli's help in turning in the ticket for a $3,000,000 share because Eli owed him a big favor. His voice got aggravated when he told about Eli's gambling problem and the fact that Eli failed to tell him about it. Then he dropped the bomb about Brenda being kidnapped. Janet was horrified.

"Stone, what are you going to do?" She asked.

"I have no idea," Stone replied honestly. "We are meeting today to try to come up with a plan."

Stone did not want to leave, but he had to go by the park before he met Eli.

"I'll be back as soon as I can," Stone told Janet.

"I can take care of Paula all day. I can even pick up Steven if you need me to." Janet was too good to be true. Then she added, "Do whatever it takes to take care of the kids."

Stone froze when he heard these words. He had heard them before.

"I should be home by early afternoon. I'll call you later," Stone said as he started to leave.

Janet stepped toward Stone and said, "Thank you for telling me the truth, Stone. Please let me know if I can do anything." Then she stepped towards him again and kissed him. It was not a friendly kiss, but a full blown, on the lips, deep, wet, movie kind of kiss.

*****

When he arrived at the Roswell Area Park maintenance shop, things looked like they always did at 8:00 am. All the guys were sitting around the break room, waiting to punch the time clock. Stone decided to let everyone know what was going on with Paula. He made a long story short, and all the guys seemed concerned, except Carter.

Carter hung around in the back of the break room, watching. Stone looked over at him, and Carter simply smiled and winked.

*****

Stone met with Bart and explained how he was trying to make arrangements for the trip to Mexico in a couple of days because they were out of time. The cramps were coming more frequently and more intensely and Stone's window of opportunity was closing.

"So, Bart, I need to apply for a leave of absence." Stone was going to need his job when he returned from Mexico, since he was going to give all the money that was left over after the trip to the Lottery group. A leave of absence basically held his job for a specific amount of time. He would not receive any pay during this time. He would also have to pay for his insurance coverage himself while on leave. The insurance was especially important because of Paula's condition.

When he finished the request form, he gave it to Bart. "I'll take this to City Hall today. I don't think it will be a problem. We are kind of slow this time of the year, anyway. The folks at City Hall will probably be glad to save your salary for a few months. You know, times are tough for everyone, even the city."

"Yeah, I know. It ain't the best time for me to take time off without pay, but you gotta do what you gotta do, right?"

Bart smiled and replied, "Yeah, you gotta take care of your kids. Wish I could help."

"Just get the leave of absence approved and I'll be ok," Stone said as he stood and shook Bart's hand. "I'll call when I'm back in town."

*****

As Stone walked back to the Trooper, Carter called out. He was working on field #3 repairing the fence. Field #3 was a baseball field used by travel baseball teams. The spring season started in mid-February. In the old days, February was still basketball season, not baseball season.

Things sure have changed, thought Stone.

Stone waved and continued to the Trooper. Carter yelled, "Wait up, Stone."

Stone wanted to jump in the Trooper and drive away, but he didn't.

"Hey Stone. How's it going?" Carter asked like they were old friends.

Stone decided to be truthful. "Not real good right now. My baby girl is dying and I'm trying to save her, but it seems the deck is stacked against me."

"I'm sorry about Paula. You know I think things are going to be getting better for you. Let me know if there is anything I can do for you. Anything." Carter was looking Stone dead in the eye and Stone thought he caught a glimpse of compassion.

"Thanks Carter, that means a lot. I'll let you know if I think of anything."

"Hang in there, Stone. My mama always told me two things a long time ago. First, things are never as bad as they seem. Second, people will always surprise you. So, hang in there."

"Thanks again. Hey look, I've got to run. I'll see you later." Stone actually wished he could keep talking to him.

"Later, man." Carter said as he winked. "I wish we could have won that big Lottery. A few million dollars sure would have helped right now. By the way, how many shares did you buy last week?"

"I don't remember," Stone lied. "I got to run."

Stone got a strange feeling that Carter knew more than he was letting on. But Stone did not have time to think about that right now. He had bigger problems to solve. He had to save two girls and $147,000,000. And he only had a few days in which to do it.

*****

When Stone pulled into the parking lot at the Southern Skillet, he saw Eli's car was already there. The Southern Skillet was a favorite breakfast and lunch place for much of "Old Roswell". Located on Alpharetta Highway just a block from Roswell City Hall, it was not unusual to see the city judge, city council members or the mayor sitting under the extremely large frying pan that hung from the ceiling.

The lunch crowd was growing, but the Skillet was not full yet. Eli had taken a seat in the back. Stone passed their regular waitress, Penny, on the way to sit with Eli. Penny was not only a waitress at the Skillet, she was also an accomplished singer. She sang in the 9:30 am service at the Roswell United Methodist Church. Her beautiful rendition of Amazing Grace made her a much requested soloist at many funerals in Roswell.

Stone sat next to Eli. From his seat he could see the front door of the restaurant.

"I'll have sweet tea," Stone smiled at Penny as she approached the table. He knew from experience that was going to be her first question.

"First time I have seen you and Eli in here together. Y'all must be working on a big deal," Penny said jokingly.

"We're just catching up on our glory days from high school," Stone said, deflecting the comment. Penny left to get Stone's sweet tea.

The first thing Stone noticed about Eli was that he was smiling. His look was completely different from the last time Stone had seen him.

"Hey Stone, great news." Eli said before Stone had even sat down. "You're not going to believe this."

"Let me guess," Stone said skeptically. "Barrett came to his senses, brought Brenda home and gave you back all the money you lost gambling?"

"Well, maybe its good news and not great news," Eli admitted. "But it could turn out that way. I talked to my man and he knows a man who can help us."

"Wait a minute," Stone was not connecting the dots. "Your man knows a man? Ain't that like 'have your people call my people'?"

Eli was undaunted by Stone's sarcastic remarks. "No, no, no. You don't understand. My man will not let me down. He owes me kind of like the way I owe you. He'll come through for us. He guaranteed it."

"Who is your man?" Stone asked.

"You don't know him." Eli said matter-of-factly. "And what's more, you don't want to know him."

"OK. So what's your man's plan?"

"Like I said, my man knows a man. He is supposed to meet us here." Eli was getting aggravated.

"Who's supposed to meet us here? The man or the man the man knows?" Stone could not help but think the conversation was sounding like Abbot and Costello's "Who's on first" routine.

Eli was not seeing the humor in the situation. "The man that is going to help us with Barrett is coming to meet us here. He comes highly recommended."

Stone decided to change the direction of the conversation. "OK, how do we recognize this man?"

"My man says he knows us and he will approach us. So we just wait."

Penny walked up to take their lunch orders. According to the hand written chalk board, the special today was fried country steak. Both Eli and Stone ordered the special. Eli ordered mashed potatoes, green beans and corn bread. Stone asked for candied yams, black eyed peas, and biscuits.

"We'll have that right out boys," Penny said.

"We have someone else coming to join us. I don't know if he is eating or not," Eli told Penny.

"I'll check back when he gets here," Penny promised.

As Stone was watching Penny walk off, he noticed Carter come into the restaurant.

"Shoot," Stone said in a hushed voice. "There's Carter. He should be at work right now. What's he doing here? Maybe he won't see us." Stone tried to casually hide his face.

Stone's attempt to blend into the lunch crowd obviously did not work well. Carter made a bee line for their table. As he walked up, he was all smiles and winked at both Stone and Eli as he sat down.

"Hey guys. What are y'all doing at the Southern Skillet at this hour?" Carter asked casually.

"What are we doing?" Stone decided to go on the offensive. "What are you doing here? You are supposed to be a work. With both of us gone, I guess they are really shorthanded at the park today."

"I guess," Carter replied to Stone. Then he turned to Eli and asked, "How's your mama and daughter?"

The blood drained out of Eli's face. It was obvious that he was not expecting that question.

Stone decided to take control of the situation. "Look Carter, I don't want to be rude, but we are waiting on someone. He's looking for two guys, not a trio."

"Ok, I can take a hint," Carter started to get up, but then turned to face Stone and said in a lowered voice. "You bought any single lottery tickets lately?"

Now it was Stone's turn for the blood to drain out of his face. He was not expecting that question.

Not waiting for Stone to reply, Carter stood up and started to walk away. He took one step and then turned back around and gave both Stone and Eli his famous wink.

"I'm just messing with you guys. I'm the man you were waiting for. I'm going to fix all your problems."

Just as he said that, Penny walked up with Eli and Stone's meal. She asked Carter if he was eating lunch. Carter ordered the special with cabbage and lima beans.

Stone and Eli were still in shock and speechless. Carter picked up the slack for both of them and chatted with Penny like they were old friends.

By the time Penny left, Stone had regained some of his composure. Eli was still struggling. "So Carter," Stone said, "Are you the man that can save Brenda?"

"Oh, I'm going to do a lot more than save Brenda. But let's not get ahead of ourselves. Why don't the two of you pretend I don't know anything and tell me what I need to know to help you?" With that, Carter sat back in the wooden, high back ladder chair.

Stone looked at Eli, who gave him a small shrug of the shoulders. Stone had no idea what to say. The life of his daughter, Paula, and Eli's daughter, Brenda, hung in the balance. He wanted to tell Carter the whole truth, but the problem was that Carter was a member of the Lottery group. In fact, Carter had 25 shares of the prize money which was the most of any single individual in the group. How would Carter react when he found out Stone had cheated him out of his shares which was worth approximately $50,000,000?

Carter could see the uncertainty in Stone's eyes. "Look Stone, I'm the only one that can save both Brenda and Paula. I'm only going to help you if you tell me the whole truth, and I'm only going to give you one chance to tell it.

The problem you have is that you have no idea how much I know. But if you lie to me, even a little white lie, I walk away. I'm here because I owe a man who owes Eli. I'm obligated to help him, but not you. If I walk away, I still owe him and he will collect later. So give it your best shot."

Stone felt the walls of his chest closing in on his heart and lungs. It was difficult for him to talk because at this very moment is was difficult to breathe. He got a temporary reprieve as Penny brought Carter's plate of food.

"Y'all need anything else?" Penny asked in her best southern voice.

"No, I think we're good. Thank you, sweetie," Carter replied in his own attempt to sound southern. He was not successful. Strangely, Stone wondered why non-southern people tried to sound southern in restaurants.

Carter started eating right away. He never took his eyes off Stone.

Finally, Stone realized he had nothing to lose. His daughter was dying and here was a man offering to help. His friend Eli had control of the money he needed to save his daughter, but Eli needed the same money to save his daughter. Stone did not have time on his side. He, Paula, Eli and Brenda needed help now and here was Carter offering to help, but Stone had to come clean.

Stone told Carter everything. He did not leave out anything. He did not embellish on anything. As he finished the story, he told Carter it was all about timing. The winning lottery number came along at just the right time so he could save his daughter. He never intended to keep all the money, just enough to save his daughter. He finished by telling Carter about his promise to his dying wife. "I promised Kathy that I would do whatever it took to take care of our kids."

When he finished, Stone was exhausted. Sweat was rolling down his face. But he never broke his gaze with Carter.

Carter had continued eating during the entire story. As if on cue, he finished his meal just as Stone was wrapping up. Penny walked up to check on the table. She looked at Stone's and Eli's plates and said, "Y'all need to talk less and eat more." Neither Stone nor Eli had touched their food.

Then Penny looked at Carter's plate. It was clean. He had even wiped the plate with his last biscuit to make sure he got all the good stuff. "It obvious you were not doing much talking." Penny and Carter shared a good laugh. "What about dessert guys?"

"I don't know about these guys, but I want some of that good old banana pudding." Carter was enjoying the lunch away from the park.

Both Stone and Eli shook their heads.

Penny turned back to Carter and said, "One banana pudding coming right up."

Everyone at the table was silent. There was nothing to do but wait on the banana pudding. When it came, Carter sat in silence and enjoyed the pudding.

Finally, Carter was ready to talk. "First, let me thank you, Stone, for telling me the whole truth. I already knew everything, but it's good to know that you didn't try to lie your way out of things. We all do what we have to do. That's why I am here. If your luck holds and our timing is right, we will save Brenda, Paula, the money, and nobody but the bad guys will go to jail."

Timing...the key to life.

Stone had always thought Carter was just a guy who thought he was a cool dude. At work, he was known as a winker, not a talker. He just seemed to always be around. Not much was known about him. In fact, the only thing that was really known about him was that nothing was known about him. He was not from around here. Nobody knew where he went to high school. Nobody knew where he lived. Nobody knew if he was married or had kids. Nobody knew anything. The Carter that was sitting across from Stone at the Southern Skillet was a different Carter. This new Carter was talkative, confident and very informed.

"You might say that I am well connected." Carter began talking a little bit lower. "I'm going to tell you guys stuff nobody else knows. The information you are about to hear cannot, under any circumstances, be repeated. Can the two of you keep a secret?"

Stone was intrigued. No matter what, he wanted to hear what Carter had to say. "I can keep a secret," Stone said.

"Me, too," Added Eli.

Carter leaned forward, put his elbows on the table. "I'm in the Witness Protection Program. I was a major player in the New York Mafia. I was the number 2 man. The simplest way to tell you what I did is. I took care of things."

"What kind of things?" Eli asked before he thought.

Carter laughed. "Let's just leave it at that. I took care of things. Now, this is the last time I'm going to say this. Under no circumstances can you repeat what I'm telling you to anyone. That goes for children, parents, friends or girlfriends." He winked at Stone when he said "girlfriends." "You cannot act or treat me any differently when this thing is over. The two of you will not talk about any of this when it's over. I need both of you to tell me you understand. My life and the lives of my family depend on it."

"I understand, but…" Stone started.

Carter cut him off with a raised finger and an ice cold stare. "No buts. No questions. You only know what I want you to know. Again, do you both understand?"

"Yes, I understand," Stone replied.

Eli was still shaken. He managed to nod his head twice. Carter rose up slightly in his chair. Eli pushed back in his chair. Carter's attention was now on Eli exclusively. "I'm not used to repeating instructions. Eli, I need you to tell me you understand the rules."

"Yes, I understand," Eli said weakly.

"Now, Eli, tell me what Barrett said when he called about Brenda. I need you to remember as best you can the exact words he used." Carter's voice had softened. Eli visually relaxed.

Eli replayed the worst moment in his life over again in his mind. He then took a deep breath and explained to Carter what Barrett had said. "First, do not call the cops. Second, you get all the money, $147,000,000 in cash. Third, do what I tell you to do on Wednesday morning when I call you. I think that is what he said."

Carter was now smiling. "The good news is these guys are amateurs. The bad news is that these guys are amateurs. They think they are cleaver and powerful, when in fact they are clueless. Since they don't really have a plan, it's tough to outguess them. I've got some work to do. Let's get back together later this evening. We will meet at Diesel's tonight at 7:00 pm. It's tough to sneak up on somebody off Alpharetta Highway."

With that, Carter stood up and walked off, leaving a stunned Stone and Eli sitting in silence. He also left the check for Stone or Eli to pay.

Eli finally broke the silence. "What do you think, Stone?"

Stone did not think, he reacted. "I'm keeping my mouth shut, just like Carter told me to. I'll see you tonight."

And with that, Stone stood up and walked off, leaving a visibly rankled Eli sitting alone in silence and staring at the check the other two had left him to pay.

Chapter 29

Tuesday

Stone called Janet as he was leaving the Skillet. He told her he had big news, but wanted to wait until he got home to tell her in person. He asked if she wanted him to pick something up to eat. She said Paula was still sleeping, but it might be a good idea to pick up some food. Stone said he would stop by Wendy's and pick up some hamburgers and chili.

*****

Now that he was home, Stone was starving. He had not eaten anything at the Skillet. Between bites of a single hamburger with no pickles and chili, Stone brought Janet up to speed on the meeting. He was careful not to mention Carter by name. He had thought about not telling Janet the whole truth. After all, Carter had told them not to tell anyone. He had even made it a point to say not to tell girlfriends. But Stone was beginning to feel that Janet and he might have something special. He really enjoyed spending time with her and she always seemed anxious to accept his invitations. Plus, Janet was going to take care of Steven while he was in Mexico. Stone felt like she had a right to know what they were dealing with.

Stone also knew that you could not start a serious relationship without trust and honesty. He was not going to blow his chances with Janet.

"Remember, Janet, I am not supposed to tell you any of this. So you got to promise me that you will not say anything to anyone."

"Don't worry, Stone. As far as anyone else is concerned, I am just another pretty face hanging around. But," Janet hesitated, "Are you sure you can trust the guy?"

Stone stopped chewing his chili. That possibility had not actually occurred to him. How did he know that Carter was not taking advantage of him? People would do anything for the amount of money they were talking about.

He answered as honestly as he could. "I don't know. I didn't consider that."

Janet smiled and said, "I wish I had not said anything. You don't have much choice but to go with this plan, do you?"

Stone started eating again. "No, I really don't. My gut is telling me that I need to trust this guy. Besides, it's Tuesday and Paula and I have a plane to catch Friday. I'm running out of time."

Timing...the key to life.

Just as Stone was taking another bite of his hamburger, there was a cry from Paula's room.

Chapter 30

Tuesday

Stone called Dr. Ishmael. The doctor told Stone that the cramps would continue to come faster and more intense. He suggested taking the pills every three hours instead of every six. The doctor told Stone that he needed to keep Paula on the three hours schedule even if he had to wake her up to give her the medicine. Without the pills, the cramps would be almost unbearable.

"Is everything ready for Friday?" Dr. Ishmael asked. Stone knew that what the doctor was actually asking was, *Do you have the money for the trip and operation?*

"Yeah, Doc. Everything is on track. I'll call you when I have the money. Right now it looks like I will have it all on Thursday," Stone lied.

"Great. I've cleared my schedule. I'm going to make the trip with you and Paula and make sure everything is the way it is supposed to be."

This surprised Stone. The idea of Dr. Ishmael going with them was both reassuring and exciting.

"Great, Doc. I know Paula will be happy to know you are going. I know I am. I was a little worried about making my way around in a place I have never been to."

Stone and the doctor made plans to touch base again on Thursday to go over the last minute travel details.

*****

At 3:00 pm, Eli called Mr. Collins at the Bank of North Georgia. He confirmed that the money had arrived. Eli told him he would call the bank on Wednesday with instructions. He did tell Mr. Collins that he was going to need a substantial amount in cash. Mr. Collins assured him the Bank of North Georgia could handle whatever they needed.

Eli called Stone and let him know the money was in the bank.

Chapter 31

Tuesday

Stone was headed east on Woodstock Road on his way to Diesel's to meet Eli and Carter. He turned right on Canton Street at the Corner Grocery and then made a left on Norcross Street. He immediately pulled into one of the parking spaces at Diesel's.

Diesel's had been an old gas station and auto repair shop. The building had been given a complete makeover and now was a pizza pub. When the weather was nice, the "garage doors" went up, and tables and umbrellas were set up outside. In December, the "garage doors" were closed and the crowd was light.

Carter was already sitting at the bar with his back to the door. Stone took the seat to Carter's right. He nodded at the bartender and pointed at Carter's Miller High Life and gave thumbs up. The bartender understood and brought him an ice cold bottle.

Stone tried to be witty. "I thought you guys always kept your back to the wall so nobody can get a jump on you."

If Carter caught the humor, Stone would never know. "That's old school mafia. It's harder for people to recognize the back of your head. Besides, if you look at the Captain Morgan mirror above the bar, you can see who's coming and going."

Stone looked above the bar and there was Captain Morgan in his famous pose. The mirror provided a perfect view of the only door used in the winter.

Eli was the last to arrive. He took the seat next to Stone. After Eli's beer arrived, Carter laid out the basic plan.

"When Barrett calls you tomorrow, you call me and give me the details." Carter was talking low. "We'll make plans on the fly. The most important thing is for Eli to do exactly what they tell him to do. You cannot be a hero or a dumb shit. No offense. Just do what they say and take what comes. Me and my guys will take care of everything."

"How do you want me to react to you and your guys?" Eli asked.

"Great question, Eli. No matter what happens, you must act as naturally as possible. Don't assume anything.

Keep your wits about you and expect the unexpected so things don't surprise you."

"So, Carter," Stone asked, "Why did we meet tonight if you don't have a plan?"

"Another great question. You are pretty sharp, Stone. Most folks would not have thought to ask that question. But the answer to your question is simple. I needed to know who we were up against. I knew somebody would be watching Eli. I had to flush them out. I needed you to come, Stone, so it would look like the two of you were meeting. I don't want the bad guys to get suspicious and start shooting people."

"You're kidding about the shooting part, right?" asked a nervous Eli.

"Let me tell you something. People have been shot over $20. Don't take what we are doing here lightly. The situation is dangerous, unpredictable and volatile." It was obvious that Carter was accustomed to this kind of thing. Eli and Stone were not.

"Did you find out what you needed to know?" Stone asked.

"Yes, I did. My man has given me the signal. We're good." Carter answered.

"So, what's next?" Stone asked.

"The two of you sit here and have at least one more beer, just like two old friends. Then you get up and go home and get a good night's sleep. Tomorrow is going to be a long, hard day. And whatever you do, don't watch me as I walk off." With that, Carter got up and walked casually to the restroom.

Stone turned to Eli and asked, "Do you trust this guy?"

Eli did not hesitate. "I completely trust the guy who completely trusts this guy. Why?"

"I don't know," Stone said. "Like he said, it's a lot of money. Makes folks do strange things. Plus, I can't believe he's not pissed about me not giving the Lottery group their money."

"Relax, Stone. It's all good. We've just got to trust Carter."

"OK." Stone decided to just shut up and drink his beer.

Chapter 32

Wednesday

Of course, Paula did not go to school. Her pills were keeping her asleep most of the time. Stone had to wake her up to eat and take her medicine.

Stone expected the day to be long as he waited to hear from Eli and Carter for the details of what would happen. Janet had called and was going to stop by and sit with him while he waited.

Stone was on his second cup of coffee when Janet arrived. They sat at the kitchen table and made small talk. The phone rang a little after 10:30 am. It was Eli and he was excited.

"Barrett called. He wants me to pick you up and go to the bank and get the money. I'm on my way to your house now."

Stone was surprised. "Why do they want me to go along?"

"I don't know and didn't ask. Remember what Carter told me. Do what they tell me to do and don't ask questions. I'll see you in a couple of minutes." Eli hung up.

*****

Stone was waiting at the curb and jumped in the car with Eli. Janet had agreed to stay with Paula.

"I just hope Carter is an honest crook," Stone said without the least bit of humor intended.

Chapter 33

Wednesday

Mr. Trevor Collins was all smiles as he jogged across the lobby to greet Stone and Eli.

"How can I help my newest best friends today?" Mr. Collins boomed. Several of the bank tellers looked over at Mr. Collins and slowly shook their heads.

"We need all of our money." Eli went straight to the point.

"Oh my! Let's go to my office." Mr. Collins' disappointment showed.

When they were safely in his office, Mr. Collins closed the doors. "Things have changed," Stone began. Eli needs all the money, in cash, today."

"Oh my!" Mr. Collins said again. His good day had just turned bad. "It would take quite a while to get that kind of cash. Plus, there are federal regulations that come into play with a transaction that large. Oh my!"

"That's not acceptable," Eli responded, almost yelling.

Stone took over. "Ok, Mr. Collins, how much cash can we get now, right now?"

"I'll have to check our reserves. Give me a few minutes." Mr. Collins hurried out of the office.

"I bet after he finishes hyperventilating, he calls his boss and asks him what to do. If the situation was not so dire, this would be fun. It would make a great novel." Stone had always wanted to write a bestselling novel. If he survived this, maybe he would give it a shot.

Eli was thinking about another possible plot twist. "What are we going to do if we can't get the cash?"

"I don't know," said Stone. "Let's just wait and see what Mr. Collins can do. Then we'll call Carter. He'll know what to do."

Stone was not sure if Carter would know or not, but it sounded good and it satisfied Eli for the time being.

With nothing else to be said, Stone and Carter sat in silence.

After about five minutes, Mr. Collins returned to the office. He began talking before he sat down. "I've talked to Mr. Howard, our President and CEO and he said that, under the circumstances, we could make $10,000,000 cash available within the hour. Federal regulations do not allow for the distribution of more than that without notification of the FDIC and the Department of the Treasury. That's the best we can do. I'm sorry." Mr. Collins was sweating and getting more stressed out by the minute.

Stone reacted quickly. "Mr. Collins, is there somewhere we can make a secured phone call?"

*****

After their brief phone call to Carter, Stone and Eli returned to Mr. Collins' office. This time Eli did the talking.

"We'll take the $10,000,000 in cash. Please hurry. We are under a very important deadline."

After a quick and muted telephone call, Mr. Collins seemed to relax. "We should be able to have the cash for you in about 30 minutes."

"Thank you for your prompt service," Stone said. Eli could not tell if Stone was being serious or sarcastic. Eli realized that it did not really matter.

*****

Twenty five minutes later, Eli and Stone were back in Eli's car. Stone called Carter and updated him. Eli then called Barrett and told him exactly what Carter told him to say.

"Barrett, it's Eli. I have the money. Where do you want to meet?"

"At the gazebo at Roswell Town Square," was the quick answer from Barrett.

"OK, when?" Eli asked.

"How soon can you be there?" Barrett asked.

Eli answered, "Depending on traffic, 5 to 10 minutes. We're leaving the Bank of North Georgia now."

"OK," Barrett said. "We'll be there." He cut off the call.

"Call Carter and tell him we are meeting at the gazebo at Town Square in 5 minutes," Eli told Stone.

Stone called Carter and put the call on speaker phone. Stone gave him the update and Carter was uncharacteristically happy. "That's great news. These guys really are amateurs. You guys just play it straight. They are not going to be happy with the $10,000,000. What you need to do is to convince them that the only way they are going to get all the money is to go back to the bank and transfer it to one of their accounts. That will buy us some time. Now, and this is very important, before you give them the money or leave the Square, make sure Eli talks to Brenda. Do not take 'no' for an answer. Do not give them any money until you talk to Brenda. When you do, listen for background sounds. Eli, I know this is going to be hard, but pay attention to what is happening in the background. Concentrate on what you can hear on the phone."

"Got it," Eli said and he sounded confident. "But do you think they will actually go back to the bank? And if they do, I'm not sure Mr. Collins can take another visit from us today."

"That's funny, Eli. I like a little humor while in the middle of a million dollar kidnapping. They will go back to the bank. They have 137,000,000 reasons to. If they don't, then we are only out $10,000,000 and we get Brenda and everyone is happy. And don't worry about Trevor Collins; there is another side of him you don't know yet."

It was Stone's turn to talk. "OK, Carter. We got it. We'll call you later."

Eli and Stone were making their way down Highway 9 towards the Town Square. As they were waiting at the red light at the three way intersection of Highway 9, Magnolia Boulevard and Canton Street, Eli said, "Sure is easy for Carter to give orders as to what we make Barrett do, ain't it?"

"Yeah, but he's the only horse we have in this rodeo, so I guess we gotta ride him for the whole show."

*****

As Eli and Stone approached the Historic Roswell Town Square, they could see Barrett and another man were already waiting by the obelisk fountain. This 20' structure was in the center of the Square and was a replica of the obelisk found at Roswell King's burial site located in Founders Cemetery on Sloan Street.

Roswell's Historic Town Square was actually very significant to the City of Roswell. It was on this site in 1838 that Roswell King, the founder and namesake of the city, stood and decided that the limits of his new town would stretch one mile in every direction. So Town Square was actually the center of town.

Eli found a parking space on Elizabeth Way. One of the shortest streets in Roswell, it provided additional parking for the shops of Town Square as well as the Historic Roswell Visitor's Center. Eli and Stone walked up the brick steps leading to the Square. Barrett and his friend had made their way to the bandstand and were sitting on the steps as Eli and Stone approached.

The bandstand that sat on the Square was the site upon which President Teddy Roosevelt addressed the City when he visited in 1905. President Roosevelt's mother was Mittie Bulloch. The Bulloch's were one of the founding families of Roswell. Their home, Bulloch Hall, was built in 1839, and was just down Bulloch Avenue from the Square. Bulloch Hall is now one of three historic homes that are owned and operated by the City of Roswell as historic homes. Uniquely marketed as a Southern Trilogy, Barrington Hall, built in 1842, and Smith Plantation, built in 1845, along with Bulloch Hall, offer daily tours and unique special events throughout the year.

Both Stone and Eli carried canvas bags filled with cash. The bags were heavy and cumbersome to carry. As they approached the bandstand, Barrett stood. His friend stayed seated, but his eyes were active as he continuously scanned the surroundings. Stone and Eli stopped short of the bandstand and stood on the half circle brick pavers out front.

"Glad you could join us, Stone. We invited you today because we know you are tied to the lottery money Eli won. I just want to make sure Eli's partners understand the seriousness of the situation and were not going to cause us problems later." Barrett announced.

"You'll have no problem from me." Stone admitted.

Barrett was now talking to Eli. "That doesn't look like $147,000,000. Where is the rest of the money?"

Eli was ready. "Listen Barrett. This is all the bank would give us. Any more in cash and they have to call in the feds and those guys will start asking questions that I don't want to answer. We've got $10,000,000. That's the most they can give. We can get you access to the rest. You can have it all. I just want my daughter back."

If Barrett was surprised by Eli's answer, he did not show it. Barrett's reply sent shivers up Eli's back. "You'll get your precious little girl back when I get my cold hard cash and not one minute before. I just hope she can survive that long."

Eli was reacting now and not thinking. He dropped his bag and took a step towards Barrett. "If you hurt my baby, I swear, I'll..."

"You'll what?" Barrett cut him off as he pulled his coat back and showed Eli the black Glock hand gun that was in his belt. Barrett's friend had his hand in his coat pocket as well. Eli stepped back.

"Look Barrett, I don't want to make you mad. I just love my little girl. We will give you all the money. All you got to do is go back to the bank with us and we'll transfer the money into any account you want. That's what the bank man recommended. He said it's the only way to get access to that much money that quick. Please Barrett. We give you the money, you give us Brenda." Eli had gone from confrontational to desperate in no time at all.

Barrett was obviously not ready for this option. He just stared at Eli.

Stone wondered if he was thinking about just taking the $10,000,000 and leaving. Stone thought how Barrett was much like a contestant on Deal or No Deal. He could take the $10,000,000 and walk away with no strings attached. Or he could go to the bank and see what's in the banker's case. Stone halfway expected to see Howie Mandell step out from behind the bandstand and say, "Barrett, Deal or No Deal?"

"Let me see the money in the bags," Barrett said, trying to buy some time to think through things.

Stone and Eli dropped their bags and unzipped them. Barrett and his friend walked down the gazebo stairs and looked at the collection of $100 bills. There were 50,000 $100 bills in each bag.

When Barrett looked in the bags, his mind was made up. There is nothing like seeing money to bring out the true greed in people.

"Give us the bags and we'll meet you at the bank," Barrett said as he reached for Eli's bag.

Eli stepped between Barrett and the cash. "Not so fast. You don't get the money until I've talked to Brenda."

A smile crossed Barrett's lips. He reached into his pants pocket and pulled out his cell phone. He opened it and hit a series of buttons. After a few seconds he simply said, "Put the girl on." He handed the phone to Eli.

Eli took the phone and held it up to his ear. He listened intently as he waited for Brenda to speak. A small voice on the other end of the phone said, "Daddy, is that you?" Eli's face lit up. "Hey baby. Are you ok? I am coming to get you real soon."

"Daddy, I'm cold and my feet are wet." That was all Eli heard Brenda say before Barrett snatched the phone away.

"Now, give me the cash," Barrett demanded. Eli stepped aside and let him have the bag. Barrett picked up the bag.

"Avery," Barrett said to his big friend, "Grab that $5,000,000.00

Barrett then turned to Eli. "We'll follow you to the bank." Then he stepped in closer to Eli and said in a low voice that seemed almost out of control. "You only get one shot at getting me the money. You screw up, the bank screws up or somebody else screws up, your daughter is dead. Do I make myself clear?"

"I understand," Eli managed to say.

Chapter 34

Wednesday

Stone and Eli were on their way to the Bank of North Georgia with Barrett and Avery behind them in a big black Chevy Tahoe. As they made their way down Mimosa Boulevard past the Roswell First United Methodist Church, Stone pulled out his cell phone to call Carter. He did not want Barrett to see him using the phone so he was trying to use the phone without looking down. He finally got the number right and hit dial. Carter answered on the first ring.

"How did it go?" Carter asked immediately.

Using the speaker phone option, Stone explained what had gone down. He started to use the Deal or No Deal scenario, but thought that now was not a time for humor.

After Stone finished the story, Carter asked. "Eli, did you talk to Brenda?"

"I did. She seems fine. She was just cold and scared."

"Tell me what you heard and everything Brenda said."

Eli took a deep breath and said, "She said she was cold and her feet were wet. Before she spoke all I heard was what sounded like running water. That's it, Carter. That's all I heard. I listened hard. I wish I could tell you more. I'm sorry." Eli was the verge of crying.

"No worries, Eli," a softer Carter said, "You did real good. One more question: Did Barrett call anyone before he decided to go to the bank?"

Stone answered. "No, the only time he used his phone was to call Brenda."

"Great. You fellows did good. Things are going to seem crazy for a while. Try not to react to anything that happens or anyone you meet. We cannot tip our hand to Barrett. He thinks he is in control and we have to keep him thinking that way." Carter was sounding more like a drama coach than a mob gangster.

"We'll try," both Eli and Stone said at the same time.

*****

Stone, Eli and Barrett all walked into the Bank of North Georgia like they were fishing buddies going to the bank to get some cash on their way to Lake Lanier to catch some largemouth bass. Avery stayed with the Tahoe and the cash.

As they walked in, they were immediately greeted by an extremely attractive, well dressed blond haired lady who introduced herself as Zoey Miller. Everyone took his turn shaking Zoey's hand. Stone wondered where the regular receptionist was.

"Mr. Collins is expecting you. Please follow me." Zoey turned and walked towards Mr. Collins' office. She knocked lightly and then opened the door.

"Mr. Collins, the gentlemen you were expecting are here."

"Thank you Zoey. Come in, gentlemen." Mr. Collins' back was to the door. He was working on some papers on his credenza behind his desk. "I just need to sign these few papers. Please have a seat."

There were three chairs sitting in front of his desk. Eli took the one on the right and Stone took the one on the left. Barrett took the last seat in the middle.

Mr. Collins swirled around in his executive chair and said, "Gentleman, I'm Mr. Trevor Collins, Vice President of the Bank of North Georgia. We are glad you are here. How may I help you today?"

Stone and Eli froze. Sitting in the Mr. Collins' chair was Carter. He had cleaned up, shaved and was dressed in a tailor fitted three piece business suit.

Stone recovered first and said, "Thanks for seeing us without an appointment."

"Nonsense. Since when do my favorite and largest depositors need an appointment? I'm at your beck and call. How may I help you?"

Finally, Eli was able to speak. "Mr. Collins, this is my business associate, Barrett. I would like to transfer all the money in my account into his."

"Very good. We can handle that. There are a few questions that I have to ask to complete the transaction. Of course, we will need the name and address of your bank. Barrett, may I have your last name?"

"It's Bailey," replied Barrett.

"Thank you, Mr. Bailey. Now, what are the numbers for the accounts you wish to have the money transferred into? But before we get into that, I would like to share with you our account options here at The Bank of North Georgia. Our customer service is second to none here. I'm sure I can match or beat any interest rate you can get at your current bank. We want to earn your business." Carter was one smooth operator. He seemed more like a bank executive than the real Mr. Collins did.

Barrett was not into small talk. "Listen, you little stuffed shirt. I don't want to put my money in your little bitty bank. I have the account numbers and the names of a bank in the Bahamas that I want the money put into. How quickly can you do that?"

Unfazed, the new Mr. Collins' smile never left his face. "We can get it accomplished in just a matter of minutes. Here is what I need. Two forms of picture ID, the account numbers and the name of the bank. There is a Department of Treasury form you must fill out. The form deals with the reason for the transfer of funds. In other words, Eli, why are you giving this gentleman the money? The form must be signed by both Eli and Mr. Bailey. I will fill it out for you so all you have to do is sign. Why are you giving the money to Mr. Bailey?"

Eli did not know what to say, so he just sat there and stared at the new Mr. Collins.

Patience was not one of Barrett's virtues, so he jumped right in and said, "Eli is giving me this money for services rendered. Is that good enough?"

The new Mr. Collins never looked up from the form. "Of course, so this would be considered income for a service rendered, right Mr. Bailey?"

"Yeah, yeah." Barrett was getting anxious. "Can we hurry this along?"

There was a slight knock on the door. Zoey opened the door and said, "Mr. Collins, I hate to interrupt, but your partner called and said you did not need to worry because he was able to completely wrap up the deal he was working on by himself."

"Thank you, Zoey. Please see that we are not disturbed." The new Mr. Collins said, complete with a wink.

Carter turned his attention back to Barrett. "Now Mr. Bailey, if you are in a big hurry, there is a way to speed things up. We can transfer the funds from Eli's account to a new account in your name here at the Bank of North Georgia. Then you can authorize the transfer of the funds to your account in the Bahamas. If we don't do it that way, the transfer from Eli's account to your account in the Bahamas will have to be notarized because of the large amount of money. We can only transfer amounts less than $10,000,000 to someone else's offshore accounts without the Department of Treasury's approval. Simply put, I can move all the money from Eli's account to a BNG account in your name. You can then transfer any amount of your money to any of your accounts without any approvals or notifications. Do it this way and it will take 10 minutes, 15 tops. Transfer the money directly from Eli's account to yours and it will take the rest of today and most of tomorrow."

Barrett was really losing his patience now. "Ok, ok, ok. Just do what you have to and be quick about it. I've got a plane to catch.

"Ok, then," the new Mr. Collins said. "To speed things up, here is what we will do. Eli, all you need to do is sign this withdrawal slip and we can get you on your way. Then we'll get Mr. Bailey's money to where he wants it." He handed Eli the withdrawal slip.

Eli took the slip and looked at it. It had $137,000,000 in the withdrawal line. He looked up at Barrett and said, "You tell me what I want to know, and I will sign this."

Barrett smiled and said, "Here's what I'll do. I'll write the info on a piece of paper and give it to Mr. Collins here. When I confirm that the money is in my account in the Bahamas, then Mr. Collins can hand you the paper. Deal?"

Barrett was watching Eli. Eli was searching for an answer when he noticed a very slight, almost undetectable nod by the new Mr. Collins.

Eli turned to Barrett and said, "Ok, but you better not be screwing with me."

Barrett took a pen and pad from Mr. Collins' desk and scribbled something on it and handed the note to Mr. Collins. Mr. Collins looked at the note, looked at Eli and then winked at Barrett. He placed the note face down on his desk.

The new Mr. Collins continued, "Ok then, let's get started. Eli, please sign the withdrawal slip and this document stating the purpose of the money exchange." Eli signed both documents and slid them across the desk. "Great, Eli, I'm done with you. Now, Mr. Bailey, you have a few more pages to sign." Mr. Collins slid several official looking documents across the desk. "The first paper is opening an account here at the Bank of North Georgia. The second form is a declaration of the intent of the income, which Eli also signed. The third form is authorization to transfer the income to your bank in the Bahamas. Please check the account numbers on the forms to ensure accuracy. The last form is a power of attorney in case the Feds require a random authorization. They often do so when large sums of money like this are transferred off-shore."

Barrett, more than ready to get out of the bank and out of the country, picked up the pen and signed everywhere he was instructed.

"Thank you, sir." Carter said to Barrett. "Give me a couple of minutes here at the computer and you should be able to confirm everything in just a couple of minutes."

The new Mr. Collins moved rapidly at the computer. In no time at all he said, "Ok. Mr. Bailey, the money is in your accounts."

Barrett pulled his cell phone out of his pocket and jumped on the internet. With just a few quick strokes on the small keyboard, he began smiling. He obviously liked what he saw. He got up out of his chair and reached across the desk to shake the new Mr. Collins' hand.

"Thank you, Mr. Collins. It was a pleasure doing business with you. I did not mean that about you being a stuffed shirt."

The new Mr. Collins smiled and said, "No worries, Mr. Bailey. I took no offense to the comment. If you ever need someone to take care of your money, you call me."

"Okay," Barrett said. "But don't hold your breath."

The new Mr. Collins went back to work on the computer.

As Barrett was leaving, he whispered to Eli, "You're a wimp. I wouldn't let anyone take my money or my daughter." He was laughing as he left the office.

Eli turned to Carter and said, "Let me have the paper." Eli's face went completely white as he read the note and he had to sit down.

"Your daughter could recognize us. We could not leave any loose ends.   If try to follow us we will kill you, too.   See ya, sucker."

"Oh my God. You saw the paper, but you let them go. We've got to stop them!" Eli was yelling and heading for the door.

"Calm down, Eli. You don't trust me all of a sudden?" Carter was back to his old self.

Now Stone was getting excited. "What's going on?"

Carter was obviously enjoying the suspense. "Come look out the window."

As Eli and Stone joined Carter at the window, they could see Barrett heading to the Tahoe. He was laughing and saying something to Avery, who was standing outside the vehicle.

All of a sudden, four black Explorers with tinted windows came screaming at them from all directions. Men in black suits, with guns drawn, jumped out. In just a matter of seconds, Barrett and Avery were face down on the parking lot pavement with guns pointed at their heads.

Carter explained the scene they were watching. "Those folks are from the FBI and the IRS. Barrett and his friends were just arrested for tax evasion. They were tracking Barrett for quite some time. They know he is involved in many illegal activities, but have had a hard time getting anything to stick." Carter was smiling bigger than ever.

"What about Brenda? How are we going to find her?" Eli was wide-eyed.

"We already have her. She's safe," Carter said.

"What? How? When?" Eli was all questions.

Carter explained. "It was pretty easy to figure out. When you called Barrett, he said he could meet you at the Square in 5 minutes, which meant that he was close by. When you said you heard water and Brenda was cold and her feet were wet, the only place she could be was at the Old Machine Shop on Vickery Creek next to the covered bridge.

The Machine Shop was the only building left standing from the 1836 cotton mill. The Machine Shop had been abandoned for years. Recently, the City of Roswell had bought it and was making plans to renovate the building into some kind of museum. For now the windows were boarded up. If someone knew what they were doing, they could gain entry and hide out for a long time. The bottom floor was always cold and damp since it had a dirt floor and two dirt walls.

"Brenda is fine. They took her to North Fulton Hospital to get checked out, just to be on the safe side," Carter said.

Stone asked, "When did you know about Brenda?"

"That was the message Zoey gave me when she interrupted us. But we had to play out the hand. We transferred all of your money to Barrett's account in the Bahamas. After he verified it, I transferred back all of it except $5,000,000, using the blank power of attorney Barrett signed. That will be enough to put him away on tax evasion. When he authorized the transfer of funds that were labeled 'income' out of the country without paying income tax on it, he became a tax evader. That charge alone will put him away for a few years. They'll find more stuff on him, now that they got him."

There was a slight knock on the door. In walked Zoey and two men. The men were carrying two canvas bags.

Carter explained. "These are for you, Stone. This should be enough for you to take care of Paula. You think you can handle $10,000,000 cash?"

Stone was speechless. He could not believe it. Paula was saved.

Carter continued. "Ok, Eli, here's the deal. We are going to place $10,000,000 in a new account in your name. I think you've earned a bonus for your hard work in this operation. I'm going to take care of the rest of the money.

I'm going to set up accounts for each of the lottery group members. Everybody's going to get what they are owed."

Stone was doing some quick math in his head. "How are you going to do that? If I get $10,000,000 and Eli gets $10,000,000 and there's $5,000,000 tied up in the off-shore accounts, that's $25,000,000 short. How are you going to do that?"

"I'm taking the $25,000,000 out of my shares. I don't really need the money," Carter explained. "These past few days have been fun for me. Kind of like the good old days."

"Carter, what's your real deal?" Stone asked. "How did you pull all this off? You get a team together, impersonate a banker, and get the FBI and IRS to work for you, all in a matter of hours?"

"To be blunt, I'm loaded. I mean loaded. As I told you, I am in the Witness Protection Program. Part of my deal with the FBI was that I get to keep a few of my off-shore accounts, tax free, if I helped them catch the bad guys. That's how I knew about the offshore accounts and how they work. I've got lots of friends in the banking business in the Bahamas. I have a rather large investment here at the Bank of North Georgia, so they didn't mind me borrowing an office and a computer for a while. And the Feds, they are always willing to catch bad guys. You just got to know who to call. So, you see, actually it was pretty simple." With that, Carter gave Stone a wink.

"How did you get the $10,000,000 away from Barrett and the Feds?" Stone was trying to fill in the blanks.

Carter laughed. "To be honest, we just got lucky with that. Avery was waiting outside with the money. One of the bank's customers that is a real knockout happened to park next to the Tahoe. When she got out, she smiled at Avery. He must have been her type. Well, he could not resist. He got out of the vehicle and followed her inside. My guys took the opportunity to reclaim your luggage from the Tahoe.

Timing...the key to life.

"Gosh Carter, you got it all covered. I don't know how to thank you. But I still have two questions for you. First, when did you figure out our group had won the lottery? And second, why didn't you just turn me in then?" Stone asked.

Carter was enjoying the question and answer session. "I knew we had won on Wednesday when I looked at the tickets you left on the table in the break room. You must have bought the extra ticket on Wednesday morning on your way into work. That was quick thinking, Stone."

Stone sighed and came clean. "You're right. I didn't think anyone would notice. I guess I was wrong."

"To answer your second question, I didn't turn you in because I knew you were one of the good guys. You have always treated people honestly and fairly. You always have a smile on your face, even when you don't really want to. But more than that, I knew about Paula and I felt confident you were just trying to save her."

"I don't know what to say, but thank you and God bless you, Carter." Stone was close to tears. He stepped over to Carter and gave him a big bear hug. Carter hugged him back.

Eli spoke up, "I enjoy a love scene as much as anyone, but can we cut it short and go see my daughter?"

Stone laughed. "Why don't we all go get Brenda and then head over to my place and celebrate?"

Chapter 35

Friday

The Hartsville Jackson Airport in Atlanta is the world's busiest airport. It got that distinction not because more planes fly into Atlanta than other major cities, but because Atlanta is one of the few major cities that has only one airport.

Stone and Paula's flight for Mexico was scheduled to leave at 1:34 pm. To get through security, airport officials recommend arriving two hours early. Stone had insisted that they get to the airport by 10:00 am, just to be safe. He did not want to take any chances with missing their flight.

As promised, Dr. Ishmael had made all the arrangements and taken care of all the details. The only thing Stone and Paula had to do was pack and show up.

Janet, Steven, Colby, and Jade all went to the airport to see them off. They had parked in the short term parking lot and walked to the terminal. They checked their luggage at the curb. Even though Stone was now a millionaire, he still hated to pay extra for his luggage. It seemed to him that at the prices they were charging for air fare, the luggage should at least get a free trip.

Once inside the terminal, they checked the security lines. They were surprisingly short, so Stone suggested they grab something to eat.

The group settled on Popeye's Fried Chicken. It was a little early for lunch, but everyone wanted to spend as much time together as possible. The next couple of months were going to be tough on everyone.

Tough on everyone, except maybe Eli. He had called Kay, from the Lottery office, and they had a date Saturday Night. Eli was liking his new found lifestyle.

When the group finished eating it was 11:35 am. As much as Stone hated to, he told Paula that they had to go.

As they were making their way to the final security checkpoint, Stone pulled Paula out of line and called Janet over. This was very unusual and drew the attention of the security workers. Stone stepped under the ropes that formed the line as Janet approached. He reached into his jacket pocket and pulled out a small black box. He opened it, revealing a rather large diamond ring.

Stone dropped down on one knee. The whole terminal came to a stop. Everyone was watching, listening, just like in the movies.

"I know this is sudden and you don't have a lot of time to think about it. Janet, would you marry me when we get back from Mexico?"

Janet was completely caught off guard. She looked at Stone, then Paula, then Steven and then Colby and Jade. Every one of them were smiling and nodding. From the looks on their faces, she was the only one who had not known this was coming.

"I can't believe your timing. You're getting on a plane to leave the country for God knows how long and you ask me to marry you?" Janet was trembling with excitement.

Janet looked deeply into Stone's eyes and said, "Yes. Yes! YES."

Timing...The Key to Life.

Acknowledgements:

As you probably know by now, I took some editorial liberties with a couple of things in the story.

First, I know little about health related issues. Everything about the kidney thing was made up. I apologize to any health professional that reads this story. I have no idea if there is black market for such things as kidneys, although I suspect there is.

Second, I never visited the Georgia Lottery Headquarters. I just made up what I thought it would look like. I am sure the real office is very professional looking.

Third, I have no idea how off-shore banking works. My apologizes to the banking world and the FBI. I am sure that moving large amounts of cash around is much more complicated than it was in the book. I simplified things because Stone and Paula had to plane to catch.

I hope you enjoyed the adventures of Stone Lee. Who knows, he might just be back with another adventure, now that he's rich.

40847093R00121

Made in the USA
Charleston, SC
15 April 2015